CALIFORNIA RUSH

California Rush

a novel

Sherwood Kiraly

MACMILLAN PUBLISHING COMPANY • NEW YORK
COLLIER MACMILLAN PUBLISHERS • LONDON

Macmillan Publishing Company
866 Third Avenue, New York, NY 10022
Collier Macmillan Canada, Inc.

This is a work of fiction. Names, characters, places, and
incidents either are the product of the author's imagination
or are used fictitiously. Any resemblance to actual events
or persons, living or dead, is entirely coincidental.

Library of Congress Cataloging-in-Publication Data
Kiraly, Sherwood.
   California rush/Sherwood Kiraly.
      p.   cm.
   ISBN 0-02-563570-0
   I. Title.
PS3561.I648C35   1990   89-39872 CIP
813′.54—dc20

Macmillan books are available at special discounts for bulk
purchases for sales promotions, premiums, fund-raising,
or educational use. For details, contact:

Special Sales Director
Macmillan Publishing Company
866 Third Avenue
New York, NY 10022

10 9 8 7 6 5 4 3 2 1

Printed in the United States of America

For Patti Jo, Keaton and Katie
in memory of Sherry Kiraly

ACKNOWLEDGMENTS

CALIFORNIA RUSH WAS NOT BORN UNAIDED, and here I'd like to thank the midwives and surgical team. Michael Shain, Roger Scholl, Sue Bringhurst, Bill Thompson, Joe Martin, Paul Hendricks and Chris Whitehead all offered encouragement and shrewd suggestions while the book was in progress. Denny Allen of King Features Syndicate went far out of his way to act as my agent and find the manuscript a home. Rick Wolff and Bill Rosen, director of sports books and publisher at Macmillan respectively, took it on and guided it, and me, through to publication.

You can't write a baseball story in a vacuum, without debt to the writing that has come before. This one began in appreciation of the enjoyment I have received from the baseball books of Ring Lardner, Jim Brosnan, Jim Bouton, Bill James and Lawrence Ritter.

Finally, I would like to thank my family, and in particular my wife, Patti Jo, who told me I could do it and stuck by me while I did.

CALIFORNIA RUSH

1

I ALWAYS INTENDED TO BECOME AN ACTOR OR a broadcaster when my playing days were over. I look all right and I can talk fast without thinking too hard. Now, though, it looks like all that is going to have to wait. I'm so tied up in the public's mind with what happened last fall that nobody even wants to think about me right now. My agent told me to lay low, go home, sit around, maybe work on my memoirs. Stay out of the picture. Wait till things cool down.

So okay, I know he was kidding about my memoirs, but I *do* have a viewpoint on what they're calling the Last Game that the sportswriters and social critics and cops and shrinks don't have. Here some of these guys are saying that if the rules of baseball could allow that game to happen, why, then, you should change the rules or abolish baseball or some damn thing. Everybody's got an opinion after a riot and a fire.

It was some game, that California Rush game; I'll go along with that. Afterward they talked to a guy at Cooperstown, at the Hall of Fame, and he said all the plaques in the Hall fell off the wall that night. I heard someone on TV say, "This is what happens when lunatics play by the rules."

Well, maybe, but if that's so, you do something about the lunatics; you don't change the rules. Baseball makes sense. It wasn't baseball's fault.

I've heard and read so much drool about the whole thing that I've decided to weigh in with an informed opinion. I knew the main men in that game better than anybody, and if I tell my little tale and theirs you'll be able to make up your own mind about what happened. It's like that guy who told the story of *Moby-Dick;* he was on the boat and you weren't, so you can believe his story or make up one of your own.

I was on the boat. Call me Charlie.

A lot of ballplayers behave like there was no major leagues before they got there. They don't know the history or the traditions, sometimes they don't even know who they're playing against. To them, everything that happens is new. But I've been a student of the game even longer than I've been a player.

I grew up in the fifties in a little river town called LaPorte in northeastern Missouri, listening to the Cardinals on the radio when the announcers were Harry Caray, Joe Garagiola and Jack Buck. They made the game fun for me right off. Harry was always singing "Happy Birthday" to people I never heard of and just about every night he'd have a new "favorite town," as in: "Carl Sawatski, now batting, is from Shickshinny, Pennsylvania . . . my favorite town." Just before one game, Jack

Buck told Harry, "Marichal was supposed to pitch today, but a half hour before game time he came up lame and had to be destroyed." I'd sit in our parlor at night while the moths beat their brains out against the windows and listen to the play-by-play, holding my beat-up Cardinal baseball cards and looking at the players' pictures while they batted or pitched, trying to will them to success from 150 miles away.

I read everything I could about baseball back then, and kept it up as I got older. And I played, of course . . . of course I played. After I got over a brief intention to be a cowboy all I ever wanted to do was play ball.

It was the cowboy stuff that almost ruined my career before it started, when I was four. We lived on a hill across the road from the town cemetery, and I used to play there as a little boy. It wasn't a ghoulish place to me; it was pretty, and I liked to look at the tombstones. Fact was, I used to like to *sit* on the tombstones and pretend they were horses and I was chasing the bad guys. I guess when you're four you can slap up a game with just about anything.

Anyway, there was this tombstone out there with my name on it—Charles, my first name, was a family name on my mother's side—and that tombstone that said "Charles" was my horse. I'd sit on that thing and be Roy Rogers until I got bored and did something else.

One summer afternoon I did something bad and my mother told me I couldn't go outside. Most of the time I was good, but on this day I was full of rebellion and I sneaked out of the house and out to the cemetery to play cowboys. I couldn't sit on the "Charles" stone because my mother could see that one from our house, so I meandered farther out in the graveyard to where she couldn't see me, and I climbed up on another tombstone to ride.

Now I don't do this kind of thing anymore, so I don't know if it's still true, but back then some of the older stones weren't firm on their bases; they just sat there and if you kicked them they'd fall right over. The stone I chose to ride on was like that, and as I started riding, chasing the bad guys, that stone started to wobble. I decided I'd better get off, but as I dismounted—on the grave side—the stone fell over and landed on me and smashed my right knee. And there I was: a four-year-old who'd been bad, lying on somebody's grave with a tombstone on top of him and noplace to go and nothing to do but yell and cry at the blue blue sky.

I don't know how long I was there. I remember the sky and how heavy the tombstone was. I don't remember the pain, but it must have been considerable. It was kind of like the situations I used to see on *Lassie* on TV, but I didn't have a dog at that time. After a while a couple of men came cutting through the cemetery on their way home from working at the foundry down by the Mississippi at the foot of our hill. They pulled the stone off me and told me to go home. When they found out I couldn't, one of them carried me to our back door and gave me to my poor mom, who put me right in the Studebaker and took me to Dr. Everett, the town GP.

The only two other things I recall about that day are that Mom bought me six comic books on the way home— more than I'd ever gotten before by far—and what I did at Doc Everett's office. He was a nice old guy, but he started bending my knee while I was on his table, I guess to see if he could, and nothing in my little life up to then had even come close to hurting that bad. It hurt so bad I screamed, but he bent my knee again, and I wanted to scream something foul and bad at him to show him how much I hated him, but I didn't know any curses yet. The only bad thing I knew to say was "Shut up"—I'd gotten in trouble for saying it to my parents once—so I just screamed "Shut up!" at the old guy over and over, which must have perplexed him since nobody else was saying anything at that moment. I've had a lot of things happen to me since, but there can't be more than a few as clear in my memory as lying on Doc Everett's table screaming "Shut up!" at him while he bent my knee that night in LaPorte in 1954.

Well, his diagnosis was that my kneecap was broken—even now I don't know why he had to bend it *twice* to find that out—and he put my leg in a cast and Mom took me home, stopping on the way for those comic books.

For quite a while it was a subject of debate in my parents' minds and mine as to whether I'd ever walk and run right again. It was also a question in my father's mind as to whether a boy dumb enough to ride on wobbly tombstones *deserved* to walk and run again. About then is when Dad says I turned from a nice, well-behaved boy to what he calls a "snot." When the cast came off in a couple months I decided it was too hard to walk and I'd spend the rest of my life having my folks bring things to me. They wouldn't go along, and I eventually got to hobbling around on my white, shrunken leg, but my disposition didn't improve. Nowadays they have ballplayers who won't talk to the writers, but I preceded all of them. I made myself unavailable for interviews when I was four and a half.

It turned out that Doc Everett, like so many of those legendary country doctors, handled unusual emergencies pretty well. By the time I was five that October I was walking okay, and when my love affair with baseball began a couple years later I was running around just like any other kid. I never had trouble with my knee again until I got to the big leagues and started pounding on that AstroTurf. Then it all came back to me. Whenever I speak to Little Leaguers I always tell them, "Boys, stay off those tombstones."

I'm sitting here now, asking myself why I decided so soon and so positively that baseball was the life for me. The first reason is clear enough: I could play it. Most of the men you meet who don't like the game, if you know them well enough to ask, you'll find out they had a bad experience playing ball when they were young. Maybe they got hit in the mouth with the ball or the bat one time, or they did something on the field that made everybody laugh, or they got picked last when everybody chose up sides. Who needs that? People don't like to do things they aren't good at. Me, I don't like water-skiing. I tried it once, behind a power boat on the Mississippi when I was twelve or so, and I never *did* get up on those skis. I just held on and lay on my back for about a quarter mile, with the water running over my face, looking up at the sky again. If I'd kept at it I might have eventually stood up on the skis and been able to take a look around, but that one experience pretty much soured me on the sport.

I stuck with baseball, though. I played it with other kids and I played it by myself, ball against a wall, until I was a good glove and a passable bat, and with my knee all right I could run, too. Football and basketball were for the bigger boys, but I was equal to them on a diamond.

And baseball had a continuity to it that appealed to me. All that history, all those old heroes I read about, made me feel part of something grand and great right from the start. Look here: If a batter hits a chopper to short, and a Little League shortstop charges it and throws him out at first by an eyeblink, that kid is doing just what Honus Wagner did in 1903; he might as well *be* Honus Wagner. A lot of things have changed since 1903, but it always made me feel good to know I was part of something so finely timed and graceful that it was still the same after all those years.

But I'd have to say the final factor, the clincher that made baseball so important to me, was my discovery of the difference between playing ball and working. I had my first experience with real work when I was fourteen, and it was a frightening revelation. It was altogether different from my understanding of what life was supposed to be like.

That summer my father, who ran the grocery in LaPorte, got me a job picking produce for a farmer named Peel outside of town. Peel was a jolly, stocky sort of fellow whose annual plan was to grow and sell enough stuff in the summer so he could stay drunk all winter. He had me out in the fields every day, with a few other kids who seemed to take to it better than I did. I'm not proud of my reaction to working for Mr. Peel that summer; I've been told it shows a missing link in my character, and I believe it. But there it was, all the same. I was no happier picking vegetables than I'd been under the tombstone.

Picking corn was all right; I didn't mind that. We did it real early in the morning before it got too hot, and aside from getting little cuts around my eyes from the stalks now and then it was almost enjoyable, snapping those ears off. But after that we'd pick beans, squash and tomatoes, and the beans and squash in particular were mighty close to the ground. We were out there bent over like Uncle Rummy looking for quarters, squat-walking down row after row while the sun got our backs nice and toasty. You get plenty of time to think about your future when you're out in a field in mid-America with nothing as far as the eye can see but beans. No prying media guys out there to check up on your technique, either; there's plenty of privacy in a beanfield.

And I decided that summer, while the sun focused its full attention on my back, that the miracle of the soil and growing things was lost on me. It was work, and I knew right away that I admired people who work hard, who toil in the fields, who pull their living out of the ground with the sweat of their brows and their groins and their armpits, and that I didn't ever, ever want to be one of those people again.

My mother suggested an alternative for me: office work. Ever since the tombstone incident she'd had it in

her head that I was accident-prone and should stay in-
doors, so the summer after my farming experience she
sent me across the river to Quincy, Illinois, to learn
typing in six weeks at the Gem City Business College.
Well, I learned it; I'm doing it now. But here again, while
I conceived an admiration for people who can stay inside
all their lives, clackety-clacking away on a Wordomatic
machine, it was just another case of "Wrong Way: Do
Not Enter" as far as I was concerned. I felt like a dog
tied to a tree.

My encounters with white-collar and no-collar work
turned my liking for baseball into love. I was a bright-
eyed little guy in my teens, and I was willing to expend
every particle of energy in my body to keep from becoming anything my folks might want me to be. So I played
Little League; I played Pony League; I played rubber-ball
baseball with my friend Billy Painter up against a barn
door with a chalked strike zone; I fielded bad-hop grounders
in our yard and didn't quit when they knocked me silly.

And the more I played the game, the more I was
impressed with how much *sense* it all made. The rules
are so balanced and pretty, all those threes and nines that
seem arbitrary but come out so pure and even and fair.
The rules *are* fair, and the breaks *do* even out over the
long season, and when it's all done at the end of the year
the best team is in first place. It probably won't come as
news to you that a lot of life doesn't make much sense;
smarter people than me have commented on it. And a lot
of us like to live and work in an invented world that has
sense and logic imposed on it. It makes us feel better.
Baseball became that world for me.

As we go on now, and you meet Jay Bates, Davy Tremayne, Fabian Koonce and the California Rush, remember what I said about my game: Baseball makes sense. It wasn't baseball's fault.

2

WHEN JAY BATES AND I WERE MINOR LEAGUERS he did one of the scariest things I've ever seen on a ballfield. Old players know the story and I've heard some laugh about it, but it sure wasn't funny when it happened.

Several trees have been cut down lately so people could analyze Jay in the papers, and I can state that even twenty-some years ago in the South Central League he was quite a conversation piece. He was nineteen, playing center field for Monmouth, Indiana, and I was eighteen, young Charlie Tyke, all signed up and at shortstop for the same team.

At a glance we were similar—short, skinny, fast, a couple of weasels. I ran everywhere, trying to impress our manager, an old major leaguer named Jensen who used to rub his face and shake his head a lot while he watched us play. But no matter how hard I ran, Jay Bates ran harder.

Who are the great "killer instinct" players of the past? Ty Cobb and Billy Martin? I think if Cobb and Martin had ever managed Jay Bates they would have taken him aside and said, "Kid, you're a little too intense." He *had* to get to the top of the pile. He was the least friendly guy I had ever met up to then, and the most determined to make the majors.

Everybody pretty much stayed out of Jay's way that first year; he was too spiky. He hated the kind of nee-dling that goes on in a clubhouse and wanted to fight anybody who kidded him, especially about his looks. Jay had big ears and a tooth missing in front, and he was sensitive about both of those calamities. And he still greased his hair, which made him one of the last of a dying breed on our ballclub. Add a tendency toward oily skin (he punched a guy for suggesting he ate at the "House of Acne") and you've got a kid who seldom smiled in the mirror. Or any other time. Jensen asked him once why he always seemed to have a sprained disposition and Jay said, "It's my diet—when I was grow-ing up my old man never fed me anything but shit." All in all the kind of young man you generally observe from a distance.

But he was impressive on a ballfield because he played so *hard*. Most of us hustled, but he was fighting for his life out there. I knew just watching him that if success was a matter of effort alone, he'd be in the big leagues before any of us. And on this day I'm thinking of, I found out he might leave some bodies behind him.

Our team was pretty typical of the low minors. We had three or four prospects and the rest kids who were proving to themselves that they weren't going to make it. On this particular afternoon we were playing Galesburg, in the middle of one of those 17–8 games that come up frequently in the bushes. I was at short, Bates was in center, and we were on the low end of the 17–8. I don't recall who was pitching for us, or how many of them, but all day there'd been shots whizzing by and booming over my head, and Jay had been running all over hell in the outfield chasing them. Center fielders tend to get hot and sweaty and pissed off in a game like that, and Jay was more so. He'd had two or three chances to throw guys out at the plate but his throws kept tailing up the line and he was cursing at himself and our pitchers and the other two outfielders and howling at God and so on, very disagreeable to listen to.

So it's the sixth inning of this endless contest and Galesburg has two out and a man on third. The man on third was Walter Blaine—Turd Blaine. He was a catcher and he was called "Turd," a little cruelly, maybe, because he didn't move very fast; he was just sort of *there,* wherever he was, just sort of sat there, you know, like a turd. Some baseball nicknames wouldn't flourish in the daily paper, so if Walter had ever made the majors I imagine the press would have called him something else.

Okay. Two out and Turd on third. Now it had been a long inning, they'd scored maybe five runs in it, and one of our players had forgotten how many outs there were. Jay Bates thought there was only one. So when the next guy up hit a high fly to shallow center, Jay waited and waited and then came racing in on the dead run, determined to get *this* runner out at home after the catch.

Meanwhile, Turd Blaine is trotting to the plate like you do with two out. If the center fielder drops it you score, and if he doesn't you go to the dugout and get your glove. He had no idea what Bates was about to do.

I figured it out just as Jay started to crank up, just as he caught the ball and went to throw it. I yelled *"No!"* but it didn't matter; Jay put everything he had into it and it went like a goddamn rocket, headed for home. There was nobody there except Blaine—our catcher was already on his way to the dugout and the ump had turned around. That throw was a Turd-seeking missile, and it drilled him right in the back of the head when he was ten feet from the plate.

It's bad enough to get hit when you see it coming, but when you're just strolling down life's highway, so to say, and don't suspect anything, you don't get to flinch or duck or raise your hand up; you just get erased. The ball caromed off Blaine's head back out to the pitcher's mound and he went down on his face and stayed there, more stationary than he'd ever been.

Now all Blaine's friends on the Galesburg team came sprinting out of the dugout to where he was, yelling, "Turd! Turd!" That surprised me; it couldn't have been a name he *liked*. You'd think they might have called him "Walter" or "Walt" just that once . . . but, I suppose, being shocked, they just yelled the first thing that came into their heads. I know it confused the fans, and it's the part the players laugh at today.

Everybody gathered around home plate looking down at poor Blaine, who had nothing to say, he was out, the final out, the fourth out. Everybody was there, that is, except Jay Bates. I turned around and saw him still out in center, his back to the plate and his head down. While they were getting ready to carry Blaine off the field I walked out to center.

Like I say, I wasn't Bates's pal or anything. There was no such creature. But I thought he could use some sympathy. When I got there he was leaning over with his hands on his knees, looking down. I thought he might be getting ready to be sick. The ball had made an awful sound when it hit old Turd.

"You feelin' all right?" I asked.

He looked up at me.

"That fuckin' throw tailed *again!*" he said.

Walter Blaine lived, I'm told. I never saw him after they carried him away.

I wouldn't say Jay's attitude back then was unique. He just had it to a greater degree than anybody else I knew. A lot of guys need a softening influence in their lives, somebody or something to take the edge off and make them less like selfish criminals. Ballplayers live in a macho world, very competitive, where the idea is to beat the other fellow and worry about his feelings afterward, if you get time. So unless you have that influence in your life, telling you maybe there's somebody in the world besides yourself, you can turn into quite a pig.

Jay Bates didn't run into any such influence when we were young, but I did. Ran into several, in fact. The first was drinking with the boys. The second was Patricia, and the third was my little boy, Jamie.

Drinking with the boys, and later marrying so you don't get to drink with the boys, and later having a boy of your own, are all levelers. They get you into the mainstream where you can find out just how little you know.

Some guys never get out of that drinking phase. I used to see men like that sitting out in front of Joe Latta's tavern in LaPorte every day. They sat there and watched everybody walk up and down the street while they waited for the tavern to open, fifty-year-olds with identical guts. It didn't really matter where any of them had been; that's where they wound up.

But when you're a kid and you run around a ballfield all day, you can go out at night and have some beers and just sweat them out the next afternoon. It's *fun,* which is probably why some guys never quit even after it stops being. They want to get that fun back. I laughed a lot in the minors.

Our second baseman was Davy Tremayne, and he and I were together off the field most of the time. He wasn't famous then, of course, but there was no question in my mind or his that he would be. He was tall and graceful, smooth around second, handsome as a leading man, but the skill he found most useful away from the park was that he could draw cartoons, he'd been to art school. When we went out to some restaurant or bar at night he'd spot a pretty waitress and draw her on a napkin, make her look real spectacular and try to win her over. He left with some of them. But Davy didn't bullshit and brag about how great he did with women like some of the other guys did. He didn't have to; you could see he was doing all right. He just *liked* girls; he'd see a pretty one and he'd get this look in his eyes like he'd just gotten the wind knocked out of him, kind of shocked and hurt. Then he'd be drawing on a napkin.

1 6

One night he saw a girl surrounded by guys in a booth at our home bar and got that look. The other players and I told him she was unapproachable. Monmouth was a college town, she was a college girl. It looked like she was having a good enough time with the college boys.

Davy said, "I'll get that girl to talk to me."

"How ya gonna?" I asked. "Wave a napkin in her face?"

"Nope. Lend me twenty bucks."

"That ain't gonna do it either."

"Yes it is, lend me twenty bucks."

I had it, so I gave it to him, and he went up to the bartender. In a couple minutes he had a tray full of drinks and he walked over to the booth where the girl was sitting with all the guys. Davy stood there and said something to her and she laughed, and then she motioned for one of the boys to make room for Davy to sit down. The boy didn't like it, but he made room. Davy put down the drinks and sat and started talking and laughing with this girl, and then he started drawing on a napkin and I decided I might as well go back to my room since he'd spent my twenty bucks.

The next day in the clubhouse I asked him what he'd said to the girl when he went over there.

"I said, 'I wanted to buy you a drink but I didn't know what you liked so I got everything.'"

Davy didn't care much for Jay Bates and vice versa. On the few occasions when Jay was out with us at night, he was always talking about "pussy" this and "pussy" that; Davy didn't like that kind of talk. I think at that time Jay was pretty much unable to speak to girls and just talked hard to hide his awkwardness, but Tremayne got tired of it and finally set up a practical joke that made him an enemy for life. At that I'd have to say it was almost worth it.

On this night we were in the Stratford bar in town— Davy, Jay in a rare appearance, our first baseman Jim Novinger, a kid outfielder named Stan something and me. We were having some beers and listening to Davy invent the "Never-Land All-Stars"—making up names for players who didn't exist. I guess we'd already discussed world peace.

"The pitcher," Davy said, "is Jack Telvley." He liked to drawl out the names he made up, and took his time, lingering over "Telvley." "He's an aristocratic Southerner from Atlanta, lives and dies with the slow curve. The clean-up hitter . . . Niff Naffner. Big and dumb, puts out his cigarette on his tongue, drafted out of one of those California motorcycle gangs. If he wasn't in baseball he'd be unemployable scooter trash."

"Who's the manager?" Novinger asked him.

Davy took a minute, and then said, real slow, "Stwint Fwenton."

Jay stared at him.

" 'Stwint'?" he said. "What kind of name is 'Stwint'?"

"The middle name of one of our most famous presidents," said Davy. "Where the hell have you been, Bates?"

"Bullshit," said Jay, uncertainly. "What president?"

"Lincoln."

"Lincoln?" Jay was getting mad. "Abraham 'Stwint' Lincoln?"

"He hated that name so you don't hear about it much," said Davy. "I can see you don't care for it either. How about 'Superficial' Burns?"

Right about then LuAnn walked in and went to the bar and we lost the thread of our conversation.

Nobody in Monmouth that year made more of an immediate impression than LuAnn, I won't say her last name, she's married now. She was real pretty and built so well that Davy didn't have to exaggerate when he drew her. She worked tables at another place in town and Davy and her were pals, they'd gone out several times, but Jay Bates didn't know that because he didn't go out much. She had on a tight green miniskirt that night and there was so much concentrated attention directed at her when she sat down that I'm surprised she didn't catch on fire.

Jay Bates started talking about how he could do with a piece of that.

"She's by herself, why don't you tell her?" said Tremayne.

Jay muttered something about her probably not liking ballplayers.

"You don't know that," said Davy. "Here you're always talkin' about how you're in their pants in the first five minutes and I've never seen you introduce yourself to anybody. I'd like to see you work, maybe pick up some tips."

"You'd like to see me get shot down is what you'd like."

"That'd be a first, to hear you tell it. Hell, I won't laugh if she brushes you off. Some girls don't like ballplayers.

I'm just wondering how a guy like you gets all the action you say you get if he can't even walk up there and open his mouth. Maybe you were talkin' about some other guy all this while."

Jay Bates truly couldn't stand being needled. It was clear he had no optimism about approaching LuAnn, but with Tremayne prodding him and the rest of us starting to snicker, he was up against it.

"Here's the way it is, Jay," said Davy finally. "If you can't walk up and talk to that girl, you're gonna have to confine your conversation in the future to things you know something about, like Brylcreem."

"All right, you sonofabitch," said Jay, getting up. "But I'm not in the mood anymore."

Way it turned out, he might as well have been selling a virus door-to-door. He got up next to LuAnn at the bar and looked around for a minute like he was trying to find somebody, and then he turned to her. His face was sweaty and kind of gray, and he tried a casual, man-of-the-world smile that came out gassy. He said something we couldn't hear. Maybe LuAnn couldn't hear it either because she glanced at him for a second and then went back to her drink, like nothing had happened. Which it had. Jay cleared his throat and looked around again and walked back to our table.

He sat down hard and snarled, "I told you she didn't like ballplayers."

"Is that what she said?" asked Davy, looking thoughtful. "Maybe you didn't set her up right. What did you say?"

"I asked her if a ballplayer could buy her a drink," said Jay, all sullen. Davy slapped the table with his palm.

"Well, *there's* where you made your mistake!" he said. "You were too subtle! You didn't make it clear what you were after. I can't believe a guy with your experience could fall into that error."

"And you could do better."

Davy thought it over for a minute. "I could try," he said slowly. "Sure, I could try it. 'Course, you say she doesn't like ballplayers, but . . . ahh, what the hell."

He got up and walked up to LuAnn at the bar, just behind her, and boomed out so everybody in the place could hear:

"Hey, babe, wanna fuck?"

And LuAnn spun around on her stool, gave him a dazzler of a smile and said back just as loud:

"Not till now, you sweet-talkin' fool!"

And they walked out of the bar together. I was laughing too hard to watch Bates every second, but he took it pretty big. You could read him without difficulty.

If he'd been able to laugh about it, at least by the next day, he'd have been a much happier fella, but he wouldn't have been Jay Bates. Jay Bates belonged back in the days when everybody wore swords and if you looked cockeyed at somebody it was dueling out back of the palace. There was nothing funny about Jay to Jay.

3

WHAT WITH GUYS GETTING TRADED AND RE-
leased and moving up and down, you spend about half
your time in baseball saying hello and goodbye to people,
up until the end of your career when everybody says
goodbye to you. You get used to it, but some of the
goodbyes are hard. My toughest in the minors was the
one to Davy Tremayne. I could see it coming but that
didn't make it easy. I guess he was the first hero I ever
had that I actually knew.

There are all kinds of things that can keep a prospect
from making it—injuries, a talented guy ahead of you in
the organization, the breaking ball—so many things to go
wrong. But Davy Tremayne went dancing over the ob-
stacles like some guy who's never going to die, like all of
baseball was set up just for him to succeed.

I never saw him hurt. I never saw him do anything
awkward. He was one of those players with eyes so good
and reflexes so sharp that they never get spiked or hit by
a pitch; they're never *there,* they're always someplace
else. The only place I ever saw a pitcher hit him was in
the ass—if the pitch was high he'd duck and if it was low

he'd skip out of the way. If it was behind him he wouldn't back into it like the rest of us would instinctively do; he'd just stand there. If he'd been at the Alamo there would've been one survivor.

And he could hit, which is the big ticket to the majors. He always had a great stroke. Jensen, the Monmouth manager, used to watch Davy hit line drives in batting practice and say to the other players, "See that? See that? Quick hands!" Jensen acted like the rest of us were just being obstinate in not hitting as well.

But if he hadn't been my friend, I would have just respected his talent and been envious, like I am with everybody else who's better than I am. What made me take to him so much was that he helped me. In particular he showed me how to handle being scared.

Fear isn't a subject ballplayers get into much. You're not supposed to be afraid. Nowadays the players say, "If you're scared out there, you oughta get a dog." But a lot of the pitcher-batter confrontation is based on fear. After all, the pitcher is throwing what amounts to a rock at maybe ninety per, and as a hitter you have to deal with that in some way. Most hitters just say they're not afraid in the batter's box. Jay Bates always said that and I believe he was telling the truth.

But there were times for me up at the plate when my brain said stay and my butt said go. The real zoomers, the ninety-mph guys, had me worried in that first year about whether I was maybe in the wrong game.

I talked to Davy about it in the dugout one day. I was kind of down. The night before I'd mentioned to some teammates that there were a couple pitchers in the league

I'd rather see socially than sixty feet away with a hardball in their hand, and you'd have thought I'd said my name was Darlene the way they reacted.

"Listen," said Davy, and pointed to the kid on the mound for Peoria, "if you're not edgy when some wild man like Swanson's pitching you're not being realistic. He doesn't know where the ball's going. Get a gnat in your eye when he delivers and he could knock your head to the backstop."

"Jay Bates says he's not afraid," I said.

"Yeah, but he's got rabies. Naturally he wouldn't be afraid."

"What do you do about it if you *are?*"

"I just make sure I see the ball," he said. "That's first. If I see it all the way, nobody can hit me, I'm too fast. So are you. And remember—you're the *offense.* You've got a bat. Make up your mind you're gonna send it back faster than it comes in. Think ahead—if they dust you off they're probably gonna come back with the curve, low and away. You've gotta let that go by. Wait for them to bring it over. If you get a hit every time they knock you down they'll lose interest in knocking you down."

I nodded, but I'd heard it all before. Davy looked at me and sighed.

"All right," he said finally. "You're such a sweet kid I'm gonna tell you the main secret to beating all this fear shit. You con yourself. If Charlie Tyke is afraid up there, then *be somebody else.* That's what I do."

"You're somebody *else?*" I sat there and stared at him. "I don't get it. Who?"

"Well, I'm usually Niff Naffner."

"But Niff Naffner doesn't exist."

"He does to me," said Davy. "Look. Dave Tremayne" —he put his hand on his chest—"is breakable. Niff Naffner isn't. Niff Naffner's heart beats about twelve times a minute. He fears no pimply righthander. He crushes all fastballs. He is the father of the frozen rope. Guys like Swanson have no chance against the Niffer."

I was impressed, and hopeful. If Davy Tremayne could conquer jelly-leg by pretending he was someone else, maybe I could too. But I wasn't sure I had the imagination to create another personality to put on at the plate, and I told him so.

Davy turned his palms up. "Okay. Be some major league hitter you've seen. Or be a movie star. Be Bruce Lee. You think Bruce Lee gives a shit about Swanson's fastball?" Davy got up to go to the on-deck circle, then came back and said, "If you run into anybody who throws *faster* than Swanson, though, you better be *Peggy* Lee and get your ass out of there."

Davy, or Niff, went three for four off Swanson that day. And he really put me onto something. From then on I was always somebody else when I batted against the power pitchers—whoever I thought would fit the situation.

You wouldn't think something so silly and, you might say, *fragile* as pretending to be somebody else would work, but it helped me. Most of the time I "was" other players I'd seen, but every now and then I'd be a movie star if I'd seen a good picture recently. I got my first home run as Charlton Heston.

Toward the end of the season I could see Davy would probably be leaving us. I figured he'd get moved up to Springfield, the next stop on the way to the big club in Chicago. He was hitting almost .400 and there was no reason for him to stay down in Monmouth anymore.

Jay Bates didn't want him around, that was sure. He didn't even want him alive. But he couldn't come back at Davy the way he wanted to after that joke at the Stratford bar with LuAnn, like maybe running him over in the parking lot and saying, "Ooops." Hurting Davy would've only hurt Jay. Tremayne was obviously valuable to the organization and anybody who jumped on him would just wind up on the front office shit list, so Jay was thwarted, he couldn't express himself. All he could do was let Davy know he hated his body and soul, which he did. Davy didn't act as though he noticed.

One night in August after a game Davy came out of Jensen's office and over to me in the clubhouse.

"Well," he said, "see ya in *The Sporting News*."

"You goin' up?" I asked him.

"Sideways. I belong to St. Louis."

Chicago had traded Davy and another prospect for a starting pitcher. It was a bad long-term deal, but I guess they thought that pitcher would put them over the top that year. He didn't, as it turned out. But it was a good move for Davy and I told him so. They needed a second baseman in St. Louis and he figured to move up faster with them.

I congratulated him and stood there like a dope. I was happy for him and sad for me. I'd thought maybe some-day we'd play up in Chicago together. It was a kid's dream, real corny and vivid.

Finally I said, "I'd give you a farewell card but I don't know how to spell 'riddance.' "

"I'll miss you, Charlie," he said.

Most guys simply will not say something like that. So I was touched and got embarrassed and fake-punched him and shook his hand and told him to get out and he headed out of the clubhouse.

"You'll be up there too," was the last thing he said to me. Shit, *he* wasn't "up there" yet. But I don't think Davy Tremayne ever lost sleep wondering whether he'd get to the major leagues.

The three of us—Tremayne, Jay Bates and me—were the only ones off that Monmouth team to make it to the majors. Jay and I took five years to do it. Davy did it in two.

Davy never once wrote me a letter in those five seasons, but he sent me a lot of napkins and eventually moved on to sending me drawings on hotel stationery. St. Louis promoted him from Double A after a year, giving him a chance to win the big league second-base job in spring training, and he never looked back. He played second on Opening Day, went two for four and by June was on the *cover* of *The Sporting News.* He was Rookie of the Year before I even got to Triple A.

You could say my feelings were mixed. Watching a friend win the big sprint while you're still tying your shoelaces can make you wonder just how much of a friend you are. There were times when I caught myself wishing he'd kick a couple grounders or drop a pop or something. Ballplayers started making a lot of money in the mid-seventies, with free agency and all; Davy was already famous and he was going to be rich, and I was still trying to figure out if I was Niff Naffner or Joe Schmo. I'd go home to LaPorte in the wintertime those years and my dad would mention to me that the grocery business was kind of a constant. People have to eat, he'd say, and then he'd stare at me to see how I was taking that news. He didn't feel the need to encourage me in my choice of career.

"Are you making yourself out to be one of the top 650 baseball players in the world?" he'd say. "Because if you're not, you're wasting your time."

"Yeah," I'd say, "when I could be one of the top three bag boys in town right here." And the long winter nights would just fly by.

Parents are always telling you you can do anything you put your mind to, and then when you pick something to try, they say, "Except that."

Of course, my folks had grown up in the Great Depression and it made a huge impression on them. They didn't want me to be a failure. All the boys I grew up with were either working in town or on farms; a couple guys had even gone to college and managed to get out of town altogether. And here I was, still fielding grounders in my twenties.

But I was moving up, learning my trade. I figured if I could manage to hit .250 in the majors I could make it, because I was a good glove. I could throw 'em out from the hole and I could get across second on the double play without getting killed. I learned that in Double A after this truck of a guy caught me coming across too slow and rolled into me. I got an error on the throw to first along with dizzy spells and nausea, and after that I mastered the "phantom" DP, which is where you're really off second when you get the flip but you make it look so smooth the ump doesn't call it. "Survival cheating." I only recommend it in case of an emergency, and a guy built like a semi coming at you is an emergency.

I learned all the things in the minors that can give a little guy the edge. I learned to bunt, to make contact on the hit-and-run, to slide, to tag people without getting spiked.

One thing I didn't learn was how to fight, which almost turned into a real shame. Most ballplayers are terrible fighters and it doesn't matter, but playing on teams with Jay Bates was like walking home every night through shantytown; sooner or later a situation is going to come up.

Jay's disposition had gotten worse, if anything, since Davy made it big in St. Louis. He was on the boil all the time, and sometimes people just couldn't get out of his way. I used to wonder how I'd do in a fight with Jay, but not for very long. It wasn't a brain-twisting puzzle. I was coordinated and wiry, but I didn't have that all-consuming rage that makes all the difference when guys start swinging. When Jay got into a mixup, he'd be so mad and he'd get going so fast that he looked like a lawn mower up on its back wheels. You can't fight another guy if you're standing there fascinated at the spectacle he makes.

I got the close-up look at this side of Jay one night when we were playing for Wichita in Triple A, in '74. Jay had been up briefly with Chicago that season but he didn't hit well enough so he was back down with us, madder than ever. In this game, on this night, comes a pop-up to short center and I went out and he came in.

Now this is a tricky play. It's the infielder's ball unless the outfielder can get to it, in which case he yells the infielder off it. I got out fast and had it all the way, so I called for it, but at the last second I heard him coming and screaming. Jay didn't yell "I got it!" like most outfielders. He yelled, "AAAAAGGGGHHHHHH!" like Conan the Barbarian. Only this time he didn't scream until he was right on me. As the ball came down and I heard him behind me I dived to my right and he tripped over my feet and fell on his face. The ball landed on his back.

I think the second baseman finally picked up the ball. I was still on the ground and Jay wasn't interested in the play anymore. He just got up and started screaming at me, like this:

"WhattheFUCKareyoufuckinDOING, you bush league chickenshit candyass motherfucker?"

That brings up the question of what level of criticism a man is expected to ignore. I was weighing it. Everybody was watching us, which is always a consideration. Ordinarily I might have let the whole thing slide because it wasn't much different from the way Jay talked normally. But with so many people looking on I felt like I had to say something back or be considered timid.

So I got up and said, "Well, you didn't call for it soon enough."

That really got him going. He was practically turning flips in midair; he was like a Fourth of July pinwheel. His glove went straight up in the air and I don't know if it ever came down.

I remember thinking, "He's going to break my nose." I didn't think he'd have time to kill me or anything—my teammates were too close by. But I just knew he was going to break my nose and I hated the thought. There were a couple of other thoughts too; I had a few seconds while he was screaming and cursing and revving up. The funniest one was, "What if I try to hit him first? Nahh, it'd just piss him off."

Then I got the biggest surprise of my minor league career. Jay was frothing and spitting and I couldn't make out the words too well, but the finish of the whole thing was, "Tyke, if we weren't friends I'd rip your fuckin' balls off!" And he went stomping back out to center, still cursing a blue streak.

Well, I had no *idea*. But there it was—Jay Bates *liked* me. I don't know what I'd done. Thinking about it later, I decided it must have been because I'd never called him a psycho or "Piranha," which was the nickname the players used for him behind his back. I'd certainly never offered him my gum or anything. But he'd said it—Jay and I were friends. And consequently he hadn't ripped my balls off.

One other thing I didn't learn while in the minors was a "way" with women. My style with girls was never as confident as Davy Tremayne's. I was, I would say, inept.

My biggest problem was starting a conversation. I never knew what to say at the beginning. One time I was in Chicago at the end of a season, on my way home, and I decided to take an afternoon to work on it. I was in that plaza where they have the Picasso statue of the horse or the bird or whatever it is, and I saw a lot of pretty girls around, so I figured I'd try to introduce myself to one of them. I didn't want to try a real knockout; I thought I'd start with a medium attractive. I spotted a girl walking toward me, a nice-looking brunette about my age, and alone. As she got up near where I was standing I said, "Excuse me, my name's Charlie Tyke and I'm—" and she walked right by me like I had no substance. She was *good* at it. I felt for a second like I was dreaming, like I must really be taking a nap somewhere.

It was possible, of course, as a ballplayer, to get laid. Even in the high minors it wasn't difficult. Everybody's heard about the baseball groupies and they are not mythical beasts. I had a few opportunities in those years and I enjoyed myself—probably more than the girls did. Speed is not an asset in everything. But those incidents weren't exactly what I was looking for. I was always on the lookout for a girl I wouldn't have to share, you know, with the rest of the league.

My belief was that I hadn't met the girl I'd marry yet. I thought I'd meet her when I got to the big leagues, if I ever did, and then I'd be ready, I'd be able to talk. I was under the impression that success would make me more interesting, and I was experimenting with a mustache.

IN 1976 I MADE IT TO THE BIG LEAGUES AND I first saw Patricia Dempsey, so that is the year I always considered the most eventful of my life until this last one.

Everybody remembers his first major league at-bat. That first AB is clear before me right now. I see the pitch I hit, I swear I can see the bat hitting the ball, which of course I didn't. And I have the box score right here in front of me. It says, "Tyke, SS—3-1-1-0."

It was a meaningless September night game in Philadelphia. Back then Chicago had usually settled like silt to the second division by September, and '76 was no exception. Teams going nowhere call up the kids at the end of the year, and Jay Bates and I joined the big club that night in Philly. It was Jay's second time up, my first.

I had always loved going to the ballpark in St. Louis when I was a kid. I thought it was heaven just to be in that big green place as a spectator. So standing on my first major league diamond before the game actually *was* heaven except for this feeling I had that I had to pee all the time.

Jay and I were probably the only guys in the park who were real excited that night. I know our manager wasn't. Fred Brice has passed away, and even when I met him he wasn't at his best, so it's not for me to say what he was like in his prime. But my first conversation with him was a little disappointing.

Before the game he called me into his office in the visitors' clubhouse. He was sitting at his desk staring at the lineup card, a little old dwindling kind of guy with his cap way back on his bald head. He pushed his chair back and sighed and said, "You're Tyke, right?"

I said I was.

"This game'll break your heart, Tyke."

And that was it, except he told me I'd be batting eighth. Just before the anthem the third-base coach, Lou Haddix, sat me down in the dugout and opened up a little more. He struck me as a nice guy. He had a comfortable gut and deep wrinkles around his eyes and didn't seem too upset about anything.

"Fred's down right now because the papers have him fired," he said. "Don't pay any attention to anything he says about life being shitty. It's just *his* life that's shitty. You want to know anything about Trask?"

Lester Trask was the Philadelphia starter, a veteran, and I said I wanted to know *everything* about him.

"His best pitch is his slider," Lou said, "but he hangs it sometimes. Uses the curve as a change-up and the fastball to jam you. Had a terrible August and now he's working real quick off the mound. Goes to a hypnotist now, I hear, so don't worry if he looks at you funny."

I stood next to Jay Bates during the anthem and took a glance at him. He was chewing nothing, like grinding his teeth, and staring out at center field where he was going to be pretty soon. I said, "Good luck," but he didn't hear me.

Jay led off for us in the top of the first and scrunched down in his six-inch-strike-zone stance. Trask went to three balls and no strikes on him and Jay got it into his head that he was going to walk. On each one of the next three pitches he started to first. The first two times the ump told him to come back to the plate, and on the last one he told him to go back to the dugout. Trask yelled, "Wait for the call, bush," and Jay yelled back his usual response as he stumped to the bench, called out on strikes. Umpires hate it when a rookie tries to go to first before the "ball four" call, and pitchers get irritated when you shout "Fuck you" at them. Jay had batted once and pissed off two guys, not counting himself.

In the bottom of the first I went out to my shortstop position at the center of the universe. That's how it seemed to me, looking up and around at a crowd that wasn't much by major league standards. I wished my dad and mom could see me, and I thought, "Now I'm going to be in *The Baseball Encyclopedia.*" I also hoped nobody would hit the ball to me, and nobody did for the first two innings.

I'd always wanted to be in that book, *The Baseball Encyclopedia.* Sportswriters nowadays, when they're being sarcastic about a player who isn't well known, will call him "immortal," as in "the immortal Reno Bertoia." The joke is supposed to be that you're calling a journeyman player an immortal. I don't care for that joke much; it's kind of a cheap little swipe. But the thing about it to me is, Reno Bertoia really *is* immortal. He's in *The Baseball Encyclopedia* with everybody else who ever played in the majors, and he'll *always* be in *The Baseball Encyclopedia,* as long as there's baseball. He made it, he got there, and that's a hell of a lot tougher than getting into the phone book.

So when I led off the third, I was a guarantee to go into the encyclopedia, although I was no longer thinking about that. The game was scoreless and the crowd was already in a light doze, but I was awake as you can get without coming apart. Lester Trask was on the mound, a skinny righthander with a beard, looking at the catcher and ignoring me. Their catcher said something but I don't know what it was. I even forgot to pretend I was somebody else; I was just me.

I took the first pitch, a strike, right down the gut. I wanted to see what a major league pitch was like, and I wanted to make sure I could stand there without dropping the bat or wetting my pants. But you know, it wasn't much of a pitch. I guess it was a fastball because it didn't break at all, and I'd seen a lot faster in Triple A. I thought to myself, if he does that again, hit it.

He did it again and I hit it.

What a sound. It was a low strike, at the knees, right over. I took what seemed to me to be a real easy, slow-motion swing and I hit it so well I hardly even felt it; it just made a little solid "tock" sound and jumped off the bat. And goddamn if it didn't go over the center-fielder's head. He was playing me shallow and the ball landed on the warning track behind him. I ran—well, I felt funny when I ran, like I really wasn't going very fast, but I made it into third sliding.

Nobody alive ever felt better than I did standing on the bag, saying to myself, "I tripled," twenty or thirty times. Haddix, the third-base coach, got the ball for me so I could keep it. Trask was rubbing up a new one and looking out at the center fielder a little exasperated.

"*Pheee*nom," said Haddix, and whacked me on the ass. "Make the ball go through."

Our pitcher struck out but then Jay hit a grounder through the hole into left and I scored, the first run of the game, the first of my career. The players felt my biceps in the dugout.

The rest of the game indicated to me that maybe Fred Brice's philosophy had some merit. I struck out twice and in the fifth I bobbled a ball hit to short and overcompensated a little by throwing it into the first-base dugout. Trask never threw me a pitch anything like that sweet one again. I got curves, sliders, and the only fastball was under my chin.

But we won the game, 4–1, and I was a major leaguer. I was going into *The Baseball Encyclopedia*. The immortal Charlie Tyke.

Davy Tremayne told me once that the first thing Adam ever said to Eve was, "You'd better stand back—I don't know how big this thing gets." My reaction to Patricia Dempsey was something like that.

I first saw her when I'd been with the team a couple of weeks. One of the players owned a piece of a bar on the Near North Side of Chicago and when we were home that year and the next a lot of the guys used to go there. It was called The Squeeze, and it was a lively place for singles back then.

I didn't go there but once or twice that first September because I was still a busher and not too comfortable with everybody. But this one night almost the whole team went, after a win and with an off-day coming up. And I was there, with Lou Haddix.

Pat was at the bar with Frank Renna, one of our regulars. Haddix and I were down at the end, separated from her by a bunch of players and girls. The first thing I noticed about her was her smile, or I should say the look of her laugh, which I couldn't hear because I was too far away and it was loud in there. She had a big smile, it made her beautiful; real nice teeth and big glittery blue-gray eyes. Her hair was reddish-brown and full and it shone in the light. She *sat* there nice, too—relaxed but erect, confident in her body, and there was no reason for her not to be. When she walked over to the jukebox I got a good look at her and remembered that Adam and Eve story.

I watched her put in her quarters and play this song I hated that was a big hit then, "Get Down" something, and I asked Lou Haddix who she was.

"That's Pat Dempsey," he said. "Ron Dempsey's sister." Ron Dempsey I knew. He was a baseball beat writer for the Chicago *Times* and he'd interviewed me after my first game. But he was a pudgy guy whose hair was long in the back and gone in the front, not real attractive. He had to be a distant brother, I thought.

Haddix also told me that Pat was going with Frank Renna, which for some reason—I suspect here the beer I was drinking was influential—didn't make much impression on me. Frank was big and burly and good for thirty home runs a year, but it seemed to me, just looking at them, that they were a mismatched couple. I thought she was too good for him.

But then I also thought she might be too good for me. I was making the major league minimum, which was better than a nail in your foot but nowhere near what the regulars got. I hadn't gone to college or invented a vaccine. I couldn't even draw her on a napkin.

I watched her off and on for the rest of the night, thinking up and rejecting a whole series of foolish remarks I might make to her. Lou Haddix laughed at me when he saw how I was looking at her. After she and Frank left, I didn't make a prophecy to Haddix; I didn't turn to him and say firmly, "I'm going to marry that girl." But I did make a solemn, silent vow that someday, somewhere, no matter how long it took and no matter what the cost, I was going to introduce myself.

On the last day of the season, Jay Bates did the thing that cemented his future. If one event can be said to have led straight to *last* year's final game, this was it.

Jay had gotten to the majors because the nature of baseball allows some little men to succeed if they try hard enough. Some of the finest ballplayers have been short on natural ability—Nellie Fox and of course Pete Rose come to mind, but there have been others. Courage, discipline and good baseball brains can make up for a lot of muscular shortcomings.

You have to have *some* talent, though, and Jay did. He could run. It helped him get on base, it helped him once he got there, and it helped him in center. All he had to do was hit .260 and walk seventy times or so and he could help your club, and that's why Chicago had him up there.

But his biggest "intangible" asset—his aggressiveness— was also his biggest drawback. He was always pushing for something more, the extra base, the borderline call, always trying to intimidate the other guy, whether it was the opposition or the umpire—who was just part of the opposition to Jay anyway.

A few years later everybody started talking about giving "110 percent" on the field, and I guess Jay did that. But if 100 percent is all you've got, where is that extra 10 percent coming from? Seems to me if you're going at "110 percent," you're out of control, and the guy playing at 100 percent who *is* in control will beat you when you overstep yourself.

This is all hindsight. On the last day of the 1976 season I wasn't thinking about *any* percent. I was just enjoying myself. It's been said that on the last day of the year you truly play for fun. Usually everything's been settled. You know where you're ending up and this game isn't going to affect that. On this day, in Chicago, we were playing just to play. St. Louis, the visiting team, had already clinched the division, and we had already clinched fifth place. The only reason Davy Tremayne was even in the St. Louis lineup was that he was hitting .298 and wanted a chance to finish up at .300.

That last series was the first time I'd seen Davy since I'd gotten to the bigs, and we had dinner together the night before the final game to catch up on things. I congratulated him on getting to the playoffs and he congratulated me on my triple; I hadn't done a great deal of hitting since, but my work at shortstop had been good enough so the papers were saying I was a possible regular for next year.

"I knew you'd make it, Charlie," he said while we ate. "You're meant to play ball, you soak 'em up like a sponge out there. In fact, of all the guys I've seen since I got up here, I haven't seen a single one who, to me, *embodies* the game like you do. To me you *are* baseball." Then he laughed and laughed. He was in great spirits that evening, signing autographs for people who came up to our table and making them take mine too.

"How's old Jay?" he asked at one point. "I was gonna say hi before the game today but Brice had him on a chain and I didn't want to get too close."

"Jay's all right. He's hitting some. You're right to give him room, though—he still remembers that time in Monmouth with LuAnn."

Davy laughed and shook his head. "I haven't thought about that in a while."

"Jay has."

"Jay's got a little courtroom goin' in his mind where he keeps track of everybody's crimes. He's the hanging judge."

"He likes me, though," I said.

41

I told Davy about the time Jay had forgone the pleasure of castrating me out in short center field in Wichita, and the story went over.

"Well, you know, that indicates a depth of feeling I didn't think Jay was capable of," said Davy. "I wonder if he's mellowing."

"He hates everything about you," I said. "Inside and out."

Davy shrugged and paid the tab. "Hey, I'll live."

The following afternoon Davy was playing second and Jay was leading off first with one out in the sixth inning of a game we already had in the bag, 7–1. I was watching from the dugout and if I'd been thinking it would've occurred to me that there were scary possibilities in the situation. The baserunner's job, on a grounder to third or short, is to try and slide into the second baseman before he can complete the DP. Now in a game like that, a lot of the guys won't go out of their way to risk injury to themselves or anybody else. But Jay never downshifted no matter what, and I might've known that he'd welcome the opportunity to get a piece of Tremayne after five years. But I wasn't thinking about it. I was just enjoying the majors.

So when the next guy up hit a grounder toward the hole at short I didn't wake up right away. Then I got the whole picture instantly; you get to be an expert judge of timing after you've played awhile, and I could tell that the ball and Jay would get to second at just about the same time, with Davy in the middle.

On the African nature shows on TV they always have the tiger tearing after the gazelle or the zebra, trying to get close enough to make that big lunge and get his spikes into a day's supply of protein. Everything happens real fast, and so it was in this case. Jay got to second at full speed, which for him was considerable, and went into his own Bruce Lee imitation—a feet-first slide well off the ground, aimed at where he figured Tremayne had to be when he got the ball.

But Davy got off the ground even higher than Jay and went over him as he caught the ball, and when Jay landed, his left foot, tucked under his right, caught the bag all wrong and he bounced awkwardly. Davy said later he heard Jay's leg snap.

I ran out there with everybody else while Jay rolled over and over, but I didn't really want to get there. I could tell it was pretty bad. Davy was squatting over Jay, trying to hold him steady, and both their faces looked green to me. When I got there Davy was saying, "God *damn,* Jay . . ." and Jay's head was whipping from side to side on the dirt while he tried not to yell. He was all sweat and the blood had already soaked through his pants leg.

The trainer shot him up right there behind second base and Davy and I helped carry the stretcher.

Well, you get the rest of the years to think about things that happened and say "what if?" If Jay hadn't broken his leg that day—if, say, he'd cut Davy up going in instead— Jay might have decided that enough was enough and maybe even have felt a little guilty, like he'd gone too far. I think it would have been over. As it was, the only thing that was over was Jay's prime as a ballplayer. When he came back the next season he was minus a little of his speed, and without his speed he wasn't the same prospect.

The first thing Jay said after that play, aside from the usual sulphur, was, "I don't know how I missed him." He couldn't believe Davy had gotten out of the way. Up until then I believe Jay only had one big goal in life and that was sticking in the big leagues. Afterward he had two.

5

MY FIRST CONVERSATION WITH PAT DEMPSEY didn't go very well. It was over at the third-base boxes before a game in Chicago in late spring the next year.

"I was wondering," I told her, "if you might go out to dinner with me sometime."

"Why?" she said.

That pretty much finished me off right there. I was prepared for "No," but I hadn't been prepared for "Why?"

"Because," I said grimly, "you knock me out."

She looked genuinely surprised. She really focused on me for the first time and her eyes got wider. "I do?" she asked.

I looked over at the on-deck circle and checked the lacing on my glove and said, "Yeah."

"Well," she said, "I'm already going with somebody."

By this time I was anxious to get down into the dugout and on with my life, and other people were looking at us, so I nodded intelligently and said, "Okay. No problem. No big deal. Hey, I hope I didn't say anything out of line or anything, or offend you or anything."

She smiled at me. "Charlie, you haven't offended me at all, you didn't say anything wrong. Now get lost." And she laughed in a friendly kind of way.

"Heh-heh," I said, and stepped in flames to the bench.

You might think my end of that conversation indicates lack of rehearsal, but it had taken me a month to work up to it. I had plenty to keep me occupied in the spring of '77, what with trying to convince Fred Brice I was a big leaguer, but I spent as much time thinking about Pat Dempsey as I did about the oh-and-two curveball.

She worked at the *Times* like her brother did, only she was somewhere in editorial and only came to the games on weekends. She'd always sit behind the third-base dugout and talk to Frank Renna, who quickly became my least favorite teammate.

I was eager to find fault with him because I thought he was obstructing me, being with Pat all the time, but really I don't suppose he was such a bad guy. I just had this bug-eyed high-school feeling about his girlfriend so I found myself disapproving of everything he said and did.

All Frank was then was a typical athlete in his prime with a tendency to wave his dick around. My attitude was that he brought his mighty member into the clubhouse conversation too much, but Frank probably just looked at it as justifiable pride.

I remember a couple of samples of his style of talking, pretty standard locker-room stuff. One time a bunch of the younger players were planning to go out and do Chicago after the game and one of them, looking at a

street map, said, "Where's Greektown?" Frank was passing by, just out of the shower, and he said, "Bend over
and I'll show you."

Another time he was talking to Alex Ennis, a black
outfielder, and he said real loud, "All this talk about
blacks having the biggest pricks is bull. My dick's in the
water every time I take a shit."

"Thanks for passing that along, Frank," said Alex.

He had also picked up the impression somewhere that
in primitive, "natural" cultures, the tribal women actually
prayed to dicks like his, and that a return to that kind of
straightforward simplicity was what the country needed.

Nothing wrong with a man having self-confidence. We
can all use some; I remember in my late teens I mea-
sured one of my hard-ons with a ruler just to make sure I
wasn't below the average size I'd read about in some
magazine. There wasn't a hell of a lot to do in LaPorte.

But my view of Frank was altered by my infatuation
with the girl he was going with. Just looking at her I
believed she deserved somebody mature and devoted
and quietly strong—like I was going to be someday.
Aside from Alex Ennis, Frank was the only bona fide star
on the club; I couldn't compare to him that way. But
after our first Western road trip I concluded that I could
beat him in a fidelity contest even if I spotted him
ten years.

I'm a loyal type; I always stayed with my high-school
girlfriends long after I got tired of them. They generally wound up asking me to go out with somebody else.
So I'd never really cheated on a girl without being
encouraged to.

But Frank was a live one on the road. Of course he wasn't married, so compared to the husbands he didn't have much to hold him back. If the married guys are going to dive right into the nightlife when the team travels—and many do—a bachelor isn't likely to be last one in the pool.

Frank was exceptional, though. He was so determined to "get it wet" every night when we were out of town that he was looked on as a crusader by the rest of the club. Quantity was his obsession; he had to have passes lined up everywhere we went, and when he talked about the number of women he serviced around the league he spoke in terms of total tonnage and how far they'd reach if only he could lay them end to end.

These girls weren't figments, either; I saw them at the park and at the hotels and I never saw Frank staring off into space all alone or looking for a card game. He truly had somebody to break his fall no matter where we were. He didn't have a little black book—he had a *big* black book. It was a photo album. He liked to take nude pictures of his girls and put them in this album, categorized in sections according to "what they do best."

One thing that kind of puzzled me was that these girls were pretty much average groupies, not always real attractive, with a stripper or two thrown in (his favorite was Frances Perez, who he said had "Houston's biggest boomers"), and I couldn't see where Pat Dempsey fit in the picture. He didn't seem to *have* her picture. I guessed that she was separate in his mind, or had a separate album—although I didn't care much for that thought.

All in all, Frank was just an example of a pretty common type of ballplayer—a standout example, maybe, but every team has similar guys. I just decided to consider him unworthy of a fine woman's affection so I wouldn't feel guilty about asking her out myself. And I didn't feel guilty; I just felt like I'd been left off the list of alternate selections.

After that first conversation with Pat, which I also figured was my last, her brother Ron came up to me in the locker room in Chicago one day.

"Hey, Tyke," he said, "I hear you're trying to make it with my sister."

"I just asked her out to dinner and she told me to get lost," I said.

"Are you *gonna* get lost?"

"Sure. I don't have to have a happy life."

"You shouldn't give up so easy," he told me. "One of these days Pat's gonna get tired of waiting for Frank to grow up and kick his ass out."

"You think I've got a chance?" I asked. Dempsey shrugged and looked around the clubhouse. Frank was standing naked looking down at the after-game spread and having a scratch.

"You do," he said, "if you can talk about anything in the world besides your batting average and your 'soul pole.' "

The team cut Jay Bates that spring, shortly after the season opened. Jay played with all the energy and determination he had, just as he'd always done, but hard as he

went, he couldn't get there. Balls dropped in the alleys
on him; third basemen threw him out when he bunted
for a hit and shortstops threw him out from the hole.
He tried for the extra base and couldn't get it. His
leg was sore all the time. Maybe he tried to come back
too soon; maybe it wouldn't have mattered when he
came back.

I usually got to the clubhouse early, and on a morning
in May I came in to find him cleaning the stuff out of his
locker. I think he wanted to get out before any of the
players came in. Some guys just want to go, they don't
want to see the people who are staying. He glanced at
me and went back to jamming things into a bag.

"Fuckin' Wichita," he said finally.

"You'll be back up," I said, to say something.

"There's guys on this team can't hold my jock," he said
bitterly. I nodded pointlessly; he was staring at the floor.
After a while he looked up at me. His eyes were bulging
a little and his body was all knotted up.

"Tell ya somethin', Tyke," he said. "You don't really
think I'll be back, but I will be. Nobody thinks I'll be back,
but I will be." He looked at Brice's office door, blinking.
"I'll be here when he's gone and when all of these assholes
are gone." He took a deep breath that made his head
quiver.

I held out my hand. "I know I'll be seein' ya," I said.

He was staring past me and didn't see my hand. "Y'know
why I'm goin' down?" he said quietly. "Because my leg's
fucked up. And you know why my leg's fucked up? Because Tremayne's a faggot."

I was curious. "How'd you reason that out, Jay?"

"No *way* I miss a normal guy at second on that play," Jay said emphatically, still staring past me. "He did a little faggotty dance-step. That's why I missed him. He's a real dancer, Tyke. He oughta wear a cape out there." He looked at me and cocked his head a little. "You're his buddy. Tell him he's not untouchable. 'Kay?"

I didn't get it. "Whaddya mean?"

"I don't mean nothin'," said Jay. "He's just not Superman, that's all. He's not faster than a speeding bullet. He can't dance on the head of a fuckin' pin." He started out of the clubhouse and I decided to walk with him a ways.

"Usually I can get what you're talking about right away, but I'm just fouling this stuff off," I said as we went out the door.

Jay got out into the parking lot and stopped, squinting around and exasperated. "You're a goddamn hick, you know that?" he said. "I'm from Gary, right over there—" he gestured toward the lake. "I don't get my leg broken and just forget it. Somebody shits in my hat, I shit in his. You think Tremayne's gonna skip through life like the flying flit from Forty-second Street, fine, you think that. I don't think so, that's all."

"What are you gonna do?" I asked.

Jay finally got mad; I was way too slow for him. "I'm gonna squash the *goo* out of the motherfucker, all right? I'm gonna *kill* him!" he yelled, while a couple other players strode by and said, "Hi." "Do I have to rub your nose in everything I say? Where the hell were you *born?*" He walked around in a little circle. "I don't understand you, Tyke, honest to God. Everything in the goddamn world surprises you. You got your mouth hangin' open all the time."

I tried to get Jay's arm so I could steer him over to the corner of the lot where nobody was going by, but he wouldn't stay still. I said, "Jay, if you kill Davy you're going to give your career a setback it may never recover from."

"*What* career, I'm going back down!" he said.

"Yeah, but you're coming back up, right?"

"*I* say that. *I* say that. Nobody else says that. I woulda sliced that fag in spring training but I thought I might stick. Now he's gotta go." Jay was really upset. "Why do you make me spell everything out? Why do you ruin everything? It was gonna be a *mystery*."

A lot of guys, when they get sent down, say things at that time that they don't really mean. Like they're going to burn down the manager's house, or burn down the manager. They never do it. But Jay was the kind of guy who likes to take an impulse and *nurse* it until it grows up into a great big deed. I had to explain to him.

"Jay," I said, "it's not Tremayne's fault you broke your leg."

Jay stopped pacing around and stared at me like I bit him.

"What the hell are you talking about?" he said.

"He was just playing ball. Doing his job. He made a good play. He made a better play than you did. It was *baseball*, Jay."

He looked at me all bewildered, like I'd switched languages on him, the way I must have looked when he was trying to give me hints.

"Look," I said. "You got to concentrate on playing your way back up. You've got a lot better chance of doing that than committing the perfect crime. Know what I mean? This is baseball, Jay, not *Death Wish,* you gotta play *baseball.* You're not through yet."

He got this pained look on his face after a moment and shook his head while he winced at me.

"You *like* that asshole," he said finally. *"Why?"*

"He likes *me,"* I said. "I root for people who like me. It's kind of a redeeming quality. Wichita's only one step away, Jay. You could be back in a month."

Jay looked around and took another deep breath and let it out. He shook his head again.

"I gotta go," he said. "I never should have mentioned this to you. Now if somebody else kills him you'll think I paid for it, and that may not be true."

In the game that afternoon I missed the suicide squeeze sign and nearly beheaded Jimmy Reynolds, our new center fielder, because I took a full swing at the pitch while he was tearing in from third and lined it a foot to the left of his face.

I saw Jimmy on my follow-through as the ball went by and he had that look the victims get in the horror movies just before the knife comes down. Then he sort of crumpled and lay on his back twenty feet from home. I ran over to him. He had his eyes closed and was gulping, trying to swallow his heart.

Lou Haddix came down from the third-base coach's box and said, "Squeeze was on, Tyke." Then he squatted and asked, "Hey, Jimmy, what was it like? Did you see your whole life? C'mon, son, ball was foul, we're gonna do it again."

I was in Fred Brice's shithouse for days over that one, and I deserved it. I hadn't missed a sign since I was at Monmouth. Jimmy Reynolds called me the full list when he got his voice back and the other players laughed about it because, after all, the ball *had* missed him, and ballplayers think it's funny when somebody's hair turns white in less than a second.

The fact was that I'd been thinking about Jay Bates between pitches, looking at Haddix but not seeing him. After it happened it occurred to me that if my liner *had* hit Reynolds, Jay would've been called up that night to fill in, at least for a while. He probably would have slipped me a fifty.

St. Louis came to town a few days later and I told Davy Tremayne the highlights of my conversation with Jay. He was impressed.

"Wow," said Davy. "He must think about me a *lot*. That's really something. I've got a mortal enemy. That's amazing. You know, a mortal enemy probably thinks about you more than a woman in love. And I hardly think about Jay at *all*."

"You might give him a thought if some no-neck crawls into your window with a knife in his teeth," I said.

"Well, if he ever actually *paid* somebody I'd be screwed," said Davy. "But he won't do that. He'd rather do me himself, on the field. Hey, if *you* see him, tell him he didn't miss me by much last year at second.

I had to make a new move. Tell him the only guys he could've missed on that slide were me and Baryshnikov. Maybe it'll make him feel better."

I didn't think it would, so I saved it.

6

PAT DEMPSEY STOPPED COMING TO THE GAMES in July. Her brother told me she was a little soured on ballplayers at the moment and had said she'd rather take a nap in the oven than go out with another one. So I waited a week for her to forget and then called her up at the *Times* and asked her out to dinner again.

"I don't think so," she said. "I'm pretty much on the shelf right now."

"Well, it's just dinner," I said. "We can break it up after the appetizer if you don't like it."

I think I finally impressed her with my harmlessness. She agreed to dinner "only," and on a Friday after we lost one to Pittsburgh I picked her up at the Times building and we walked across the river into the Loop to eat.

Pat did most of the talking, which was fine with me. She felt like she had to explain why she didn't want to date anybody, so she told me about her past a little bit.

"Going out with Frank was a reaction in the first place," she said while we waited for the fish dish. "Before that I was with a nice, intelligent, sensitive guy,

Paul, who works at the paper. A real liberated male. But he was *too* sensitive. *Too* open. I thought I wanted emotional honesty, but he cried more than *I* did. Sometimes we used to cry together but I just couldn't keep up. So finally I thought it would be a nice change to date somebody a little more macho, against the grain—a throwback. And Frank was so prehistoric I couldn't resist."

"If you wanted a throwback," I asked, "why did you throw him back?"

She looked kind of sad. "I guess I overcompensated, I don't know. I think Frank saw me as the 'good' girl he was with when he wasn't having his real fun. He didn't say or do much when we were together. From what I hear he saved up all his wild, interesting side for the road."

She smiled at me. "What do women want, huh? What do *I* want? Nothing much. Just a strong, intelligent, attentive, passionate but gentle lover who's secure in himself but devoted to me without being dependent, domineering or demanding."

She sure had *me* pinned down. I said, "I can do the 'devoted' part. When I heard you'd left the park for the last time I went outside and stood for fifteen minutes looking at your skid marks."

After dinner we walked down Michigan to the lakeshore and back before I took her home to her apartment. She asked me about myself, where I came from and all, and I asked her what she wanted to do with her life. She said she was going to write someday—"just short pieces, I think I'm a singles hitter"—and maybe have a family. I didn't notice anything else but her; she had to stop me from crossing against the light.

And that was our first date. She liked it enough to try it again, and now, after all these years, sometimes we take time out from our busy schedules just to have a quiet night to ourselves and sit together and play a little game where we try to figure out what in the world it was we ever saw in each other.

Pat's theory is that all her life she took up with one man just because he was different from the other ones, and she'd never known anybody before who pronounced the word "caution" like it was "cortion." Mine is that I was so impressed with the idea of dating a good-looking woman writer that it blinded me to her mean streak. She says it wasn't boy meets girl; it was hick meets hack.

Some teams are contenders year after year, and others are just perennial dogmeat. In my early years in the big leagues, Davy Tremayne's St. Louis club was always right there, at or near the top. Chicago, my team, was the one the good clubs counted on to give them two out of three when they needed it. Seemed like we were *always* sixteen games out, even in April. We had enough push to stay out of last place but that was about it. When I joined a contender in my last season it was like playing on a more advanced planet.

In a way it was good for me, because I got a lot of playing time in Chicago, where I wouldn't have if I'd been in Pittsburgh or Philly or St. Louis or New York. And the fans in Chicago were always kind. The Chicago fans, and I don't mean this in a bad way, were like minor league fans; they really *adopted* their players and rooted for

them no matter what, like the fans do in the minors. I
don't know why; God knows we weren't the most de-
serving bunch of ballplayers ever assembled. But we
hustled, and I think they appreciated that.

At Wrigley Field, where we played, the fans are always right there close to you. It's an old, intimate park.
When you're in the on-deck circle the fans in the boxes
are practically in your lap, so you have no trouble catch-
ing it if they've got some comment to offer.

Every now and then one or more of them would get a
little frustrated. One day there was this guy, I guess he'd
just suffered too much for too long. All afternoon the
poor dink had been rooting with all the heart he had,
especially for me; it was "C'mon, Charlie!" and "You can
do it, Charlie!" and "You'll get 'im next time, Charlie!"
But on this day it wasn't happening; I didn't have a clue at
the plate.

We were blown out by the eighth and I was on deck
when I happened to look over. The guy had just stood up
from his seat, and I swear there were tears in his eyes.
He had his team jacket on his arm. He stood there and
stared at me with his face all scrunched up, a big, pudgy
fella, and finally, with his voice cracking, sobbed out,
"TYKE—YOU *SUCK!*" And he shook his head, saddest
guy in town, and walked up the steps and out of sight.
Never came back that I know of.

There aren't many jobs in life that are that open to the
criticism of the man on the street. I thought at the time
that if I'd followed Mom's advice and gone into some kind
of office work, that guy would never have known that I
sucked—or at least he probably wouldn't have walked up

to my desk and told me so. On the other hand, he wouldn't have been *rooting* so hard for me, either. He knew his baseball, I'll say that. He put his finger on my problem that day.

I never had the kind of skills that assured me of a job from year to year. I never made the All-Star team and we never won anything, so a lot of the time I was concentrating so hard on hanging on to the spot I had and trying to improve myself that I forgot how happy I was.

But I was happy. My God, you can't do anything as a young man that's as much fun as playing major league baseball, not if you're like me. Sometimes I'd be out at short on a beautiful night in some city with the fans stacked up to the sky and the organ music going and everybody buzzing, and I'd think about the ballfield outside LaGrange, with the crowd of forty and the hole in my glove where the thumb wore through and the mosquitoes and the lights with the bulbs burned out, and I'd say to myself, "It's just the same. I still get to do it."

Baseball was just as old and substantial and important and basic as the Mississippi River to me, and it flowed along in just the same way. When I stood out at shortstop, I was standing in the center of the fullest life I could live.

Sometimes, though, I felt a little out of place on that team, like I was old-fashioned. Some old-time players say that back in the earlier times all they ever did was talk and think about baseball, and maybe I would have fit in better then. It seemed like baseball was a secondary subject for a lot of the guys on our Chicago team. The players seemed to split into different interest groups.

We had womanizers, like Frank; we had a couple druggies, like the guy everybody got to calling "George Herman," who said cocaine helped them concentrate; we had some born-agains, who said it was God's will if we lost. Between the boys who held chapel and the ones who snorted a line or two to ease the pressure, we had a real "praise the Lord and pass the ammunition" kind of club.

I didn't exactly fit into either group. I never thought God took any kind of personal interest in the standings. I *know* He couldn't have cared about my average. I went along with the guys who prayed not to get hurt out there and that was about the extent of my religious fervor.

And I got to see a few of the fellas load up at a party or two, which alarmed me. They'd get to talking so much they couldn't seem to stop. The main effect of cocaine I noticed was that the guys who did it said twice as much as they had to say.

One time I was at a get-together with some players at "George Herman's" apartment on the North Side. George and Lonnie Frett, one of our starters, were in and out of the bedroom periodically that evening and they got into a very animated discussion. I remember it because it was unusual, being about baseball.

Lonnie was what you call a "hard-luck" pitcher. He was a sinker-baller with good stuff but his record was always something like 10–14. He lost a lot of one-run games. Lonnie felt it was unfair, that it was cheap hits that were beating him. And on this night he told George Herman about the Solidity Index.

"Pitchers' stats are bullshit," he said. "They oughta have a special radar gun that computes how solidly every ball is hit, where 1.0 is a line drive and .000001 is a foul tip. Then my agent could say, 'Lonnie Frett's one of the best in the league—he's got a point-two-eight Solidity Index.'"

Alex Ennis, the outfielder, and I were listening to this and drinking some beer. Alex said, "What if the guy hits it solid off the handle and bloops it over little Tyke's head? What's your Solidity Index?"

"Shut up, Ennis, I'm tryin' to make a point. Someday they're gonna have a gun that measures all that but it'll be too late for me. Nobody's ever gonna know how good I was. I'll be runnin' a Farm 'n Fleet in Rockford with my brother." He got a stricken look picturing it.

George Herman got all excited about the Solidity Index. He was a pinch-hitter and figured it could measure how hard he hit the ball. George asked Lonnie a bunch of questions about the "SI" and then he said, "Maybe you got somethin' there, Frett. Maybe we should call the commissioner's office with this."

"Yeah, and maybe you should tell him to come on over and line a few up on the mirror and discuss it," said Alex.

"Don't get on me about blow, man," said George. "I don't jump in your shit about beer."

Alex took a sip and said, "Beer's legal."

George jumped on that one; he was all prepared.

"It wasn't in the twenties! It wasn't in the twenties! Booze was illegal and Babe Ruth did it all the time! Ain't no difference between Babe Ruth then and me now!"

That struck Alex funny. He had a real deep laugh, and he just got going and shaking his head for a minute, sitting there. Then he said, "Man, if you can't find, in your mind, any difference between you and Babe Ruth, you are hi-i-i-i-gh . . ." He sang "high," like middle C.

"You don't like the party you can go, Ennis," said George.

Alex smiled and sighed and got up. "You are a sorry mother*fuck*er, you know that?" he said amiably. "You could be the state fool. Should call you George Herman, man, Return of the Babe." He left laughing, and George Herman was born.

A few days later Lonnie Frett started for us and in the first inning he threw one of those long balls that snap your neck if you bother to follow it. Jeffrey Barnes of L.A. hit it, lefthanded, and it got out of the park faster than any ball I'd ever seen. It crossed Sheffield on a high line and whammed into somebody's apartment balcony; then it rattled around like a pinball for an hour or so. I was surprised it didn't go through the building and out the other side.

In the dugout after the inning, Alex walked up to Frett and said, "I'm new at this, Lon, but if I was writin' your SI I'd give that a one-point-oh with a 'Holy Shit!' after it."

A little while after that guys started getting busted and suspended and going into programs over cocaine and that seemed to break up a lot of parties. I don't know if some guys played better on it or not. George Herman was through at thirty-two; he might've been through no matter what he did.

Maybe they'll have that Solidity Index someday; I wouldn't be shocked. If they do, Lonnie Frett can read about it in Rockford and moan, because he's long gone too.

If players' careers were all different shots on the Great Dartboard of Baseball, you could say Davy Tremayne stuck in the bull's-eye and Jay Bates stuck right on the edge for a while and then fell on the floor.

While I was establishing myself as a big leaguer I kept track of Jay in the *Sporting News* Triple A section. Sometimes I checked the front page of the daily paper too, to see if Tremayne had been found in the trunk of somebody's car outside a St. Louis restaurant, but I finally left off doing that. Jay had apparently made up his mind to exhaust every possibility of returning to the majors and meeting Davy on equal turf before he considered other alternatives.

Jay treaded water at Wichita for a couple years, hitting in the .250s, a shade too low to get the big club interested again. His stolen bases were down and he was getting too old to be a real prospect anymore.

At spring training in Arizona my fourth year up, Jay was there to attempt the jump again. He knew it was his last try. Lee Rabe was the manager by that time, a good baseball man, and he liked Jay's style, but he couldn't get around that missing speed down the line.

Jay was a *smart* player, though. He'd always been heads-up, but the added years in the minors had given him absolute knowledge of how to shake up the opposition. In the right spot he could get us a run nobody else could.

In one exhibition game that spring, when he was on first and I was on third with two out, he got me home by simply taking a stroll. When the other team's rookie pitcher went into his stretch, Jay walked off first and didn't stop, just kept trudging toward second like he was going through a hotel lobby.

The pitcher's teammates started yelling at him to throw it to first or throw it to second or hold on to it. He didn't know what to do. Maybe he thought he'd balked. He just stared while Jay walked halfway to second and stopped and stared back. I started inching down the line from third.

Then Jay broke for second, the pitcher threw there and I took off for the plate. Jay stopped again. The second baseman threw home too late to get me and the catcher threw back to second too late to get Jay.

It was a truly snotty play, and Jay picked the right kid to do it to. Rabe knew it was a good play in that spot, and I think it stuck in his mind when he talked to Kramer, the general manager, about personnel moves. When it came time to give Jay the bad news at the end of training Rabe had an offer for him.

Jay later told me he was sure he was gone when he got the message to go to Rabe's office, and he had no intention of going back to Wichita again. But Rabe already knew that and he said, "Look here: We aren't going to be able to use you as a player. How about if we use your brains?"

He offered Jay a job helping Jensen out back down at the bottom of the chain, in Monmouth. Jensen was about worn to the nub and had said he didn't know if he wanted to go through another season watching the bushers fall over themselves. If Jay could instruct the young players in the art of winning without tearing their parts off, he could replace the old guy.

You might think it was strange, giving a managerial chance to somebody as, oh, excitable as Jay, but I think they figured if he could file down his fangs he had a lot going for him otherwise—youth, energy, baseball intelligence and total dedication. The only question, really, was whether he could stand it, just watching and not playing. And if he couldn't, well, little was lost. They'd get somebody else. There were plenty of guys who could teach the ABCs. But if Jay *could* manage, he could add fire to the fundamentals.

I heard about this in a hurry because Jay didn't accept the offer. He didn't know what to do, so he asked Rabe for a night to think on it and asked me to help him. I sat in Jay's room till 1:00 A.M. while he walked in little circles and eights and went over every other roster in the big leagues looking for one he could make. Then he asked me what I thought he should do.

That's one good reason *I* never wanted to be a manager. They're always having to say things to kids like, "Have you considered the military?" I didn't even know if I had the right advice in me. Guys like Jay have so much drive that you could be wrong any time you tell them they can't do what they'd die to do, and Jay wanted to *play*. I just wasn't sure I knew the right thing to say, so I said the one thing I *did* know.

"You've lost a step," I told him.

"A step and a half, and we know why," he said. "I did it your way, pal. I busted my ass to get back here and now I'm done, ain't I? Tremayne's still Cover Boy and I can't get my picture on a fuckin' gum card."

"You still on that?"

"See him in my dreams, you wanta know the truth," said Jay, lighting one cigarette from another.

"You want to beat him, that's okay," I said. "You want to talk like you did a few years ago I don't want to hear about it."

He laughed shortly. "Scares the little Tyke."

I got up.

"Jay, I don't know what to tell you. I just know about ball, I don't know jack shit about your dreams."

I started to go. I was about done with Jay at that point. He was one of those people you can't really file under "friend" or "acquaintance"; he came more under "How did I get mixed up with *this* guy?" I'd always admired him as a ballplayer but personally he wore me out.

When I was at the door he said, "Charlie, how in the hell am I going to beat him?"

Oh, well. He called me Charlie, that was a first. And he sounded hopeless or lost or something. We'd been bushers together. If I'd kept going, our relationship would have ended right there. No Last Game, or at least not the one that happened.

I stopped and said, "Well, *can* you manage a ballclub?"

He stared at me. "Hell, yes."

"So what are your choices, Jay? You take the job and maybe work your way back up where you want to be, or you quit and follow Tremayne around trying to get a clear shot."

Jay looked at my stomach like it was a crystal ball. "By the time I get back up he'll be gone," he said.

"Maybe not," I said. "Either way *you'll* be all right."

Jay kept staring at my center. Finally he said, "I have a system of signs in my head, they're impossible to steal. You could have a camera on me for the rest of your life and never figure them out."

He sat for a few moments, not moving that I could see, and then said, "That's the hit-and-run."

Maybe in the Twilight Zone it is, I thought. I took him at his word, though, and broke for home.

7

PAT AND I HAD ALREADY BEEN MARRIED ABOUT
six months when Jay took the Monmouth job. I'm
not going to discuss our first kiss and so on because Pat
already wrote down the details in an anthology book
where various women relived their first romantic experience with their husbands in print. The book's called
Sweet Mystery, and it's an eye-opener. She really built
me up; I must have been a man of fire that night.

At the wedding my best man was Davy Tremayne and
my ushers were Alex Ennis, Lou Haddix, Lee Rabe and
Pat's brother, Ron. It was in Chicago right after my third
season, and there were friends of the bride from the
paper and friends of the groom from the team.

Davy was a big hit at the reception. He was there with
a stewardess and signing autographs for Pat's friends.
When it came time for the best man to make a toast he
got up and said, "To the bride and groom. Now let's get
out on the floor and break some heads."

Pat and I had to dance first, of course, and I was more
worried about that than about getting married. All I really
knew about dancing was the time step, because when I

was six my mother enrolled me as the only boy in Miss Cottrell's tap-dancing class up on the second floor of the firehouse back in LaPorte. And tap, you know, went into a decline in popularity right around then. To this day I've never been in a spot where my clickety toes were required to save the party.

Pat had rehearsed me some in a more contemporary style. "There is no reason," she said, "why a shortstop shouldn't be able to dance," but I had taken several years to learn the moves at short and they didn't include twirling the second baseman. The only time the whole wedding day that I was really sweaty was doing this disco-type thing with Pat at the reception. Alex Ennis came up to me afterward and said, "You're a regular Buddy Ebsen out there."

Soon after that Pat got pregnant and wanted to have the baby this new natural way, where the husband is in on the whole thing and even assists in the delivery. I thought it would be best if when it arrived I was in another room, but I didn't say so.

When I told Lou Haddix in spring training that I was going to be a coach myself, he stared at me and said, "Boy, you got guts. I wouldn't do that with a gun to my head. When Maxine had her first I stayed in the waiting room and watched *Four for Texas*. When it was over I watched *Five Minutes to Live By* and then I watched the test pattern. *That's* what the daddy does. You don't want to be in there, Charlie. What are you gonna do in there?"

"I'm going to help her with the breathing and—I don't know. I got to take these classes with her."

Haddix shook his head. "You got to be a man, Charlie. Lay down the law. Tell her you're a coward."

Ron Dempsey was just the other way about it, one of these boys it chills your bones to listen to.

"It's the greatest," he said. "When Emily had hers I videotaped the whole thing. There is no more fulfilling, I would say almost mystical experience. And the bonding, of course, that's very important—if you're there you can bond with the baby right away. You doing a home birth?"

I started thinking these Dempseys were a much more rugged bunch than the Tykes. My dad said he gave Mom all the room she needed when I was born and Mom wanted it that way. But I practically had to get down on my knees and beg Pat not to do the whole thing at our apartment with me and a midwife. We finally agreed that she'd have it in the labor-delivery room down the hall at the doctor's office.

Other guys might say, "I woulda told her no way, it's gotta be the hospital," but I think they'd be wrong. It's the woman who has to do it, and if she finds it easier swinging from the chandelier a good coach mans the net.

So the season started and went along, and we went to the birthing classes when the team was home. They were all right and encouraging and the teacher explained about the breathing, but they showed a movie I wished I'd missed.

The baby was due in August and Pat worried that the team would be on the road when she went into labor, but as it turned out we were home. Pat was all out of sorts that night. For most of the nine months she'd been pretty happy, exercising and eating all these vegetables for the baby and having showers with her friends and so on. But she'd gotten weary of waiting and tired of being fat and tired of me, for some reason. She got a little mad at me that night because she thought I wasn't enthusiastic enough about the classes. She thought she'd never have the baby, or that she'd have it and stay fat for the rest of her life.

I wasn't doing too well myself. I was about four for forty and my average was down under .260 for the first time all year. That very day I'd gotten picked off second base by the Pittsburgh catcher. When I came back to the dugout Haddix mimed pulling his head off his neck and shoving it up his butt.

So what with one thing and another we didn't get much sleep that night and then about six in the morning Pat shook me and said, "Let's go." She'd been up about an hour already and waited for me to get a little more rest.

We got to the doctor's in about twenty minutes and went into the labor-delivery room, where there was a midwife who was real nice and got Pat settled on the bed. It was like a bedroom. She told Pat to get comfortable any way she wanted, and sat down and started reading a book. Then the doctor came in and said hello and looked at Pat and left. He was somewhere else almost the whole time.

After a couple hours Pat said it was easier than she'd thought it would be. Then it got harder. It lasted ten hours, but it seemed like a bad week. I'd do the breathing part with her when the pains came and lie on the bed with her in between, or go get little ice chips and give them to her. She wanted a lot of ice. As time went by she had more pain and got sweaty and more determined, but we didn't seem to be making much progress.

It got to be this rhythm that just went on. There'd be a little rest, then a rising wave of pain for her that would peak and slowly go away. I remember thinking two things by the eighth or ninth hour: One was that pretty soon I'd make them give her some anesthetic, and the other was that it would never end. I stopped expecting a baby. I thought we'd just keep doing this forever.

Then it got toward the finish and Pat got ferocious. I was supposed to be the athlete, but she gave more of a physical performance than any I ever saw on a ballfield. She was this way and that way, pushing; sometimes she squatted down beside the bed and about flipped it over. She was totally concentrated—the midwife and I and everything else in the world were gone.

The doctor came in at the end, all cheery and relaxed, and talked her through the last pushing. She was finishing up on her side on the bed, with me on my knees beside her and him waiting at the foot.

And finally, there was the top of the baby's head, its hair, blackish-purple and wet. It appeared and disappeared and the doctor told her to push another extra time past when she thought she could. She did, and the head came out, and the doctor pulled the baby's arms out. He told me to do the rest and I did, and out it came real easy, crying in my lap.

The doctor said, "Tell her what she's got."

I looked down. I'll never forget it. I can't recall any other time in my life when I didn't think a little bit about what I was going to say when I said something. When I wasn't conscious of myself in some way. But I looked down at Jamie and I saw his little dick and I blurted out, "It's a boy!" I was so amazed. It was a baby. We'd done all that and here was a baby, after all.

I gave him to Pat and her face was split wide open. The doctor told me to go clean myself off, so I did, and came right back and held Jamie for a minute. He grabbed my finger hard. Pat was sitting there happy and pepped up as if she was at a party.

I went and called Lee Rabe at Wrigley Field. It was a little past four, and the guys had won without me. I talked to Rabe and Lou Haddix and Alex Ennis and told them all, "I pulled him out!" Haddix was astonished.

Then I went out into the parking lot and cried. It was a pretty day. I walked over to a dumpster and saw a paper with the sports page sticking out at the top. It said we were still in fifth place, sixteen games out. When Jamie got old enough to hear the story and learn it, he'd always do the ending himself, saying to me, "And that was your happiest day. Right, Dad?"

They got to paying us a lot of money there, in the first free-agent years. When the reserve clause went some people said baseball would be ruined because the rich teams would buy all the best players. They tried, too. But nobody was able to figure out who the best players were. As soon as somebody had a good year he got paid like he'd do it forever. Next thing the owners knew their glossy new free agent had a sore arm or a busted ankle or just fizzled, and they were paying him till the turn of the century for nothing.

It was great for us, though. The multiyear contracts were the nicest thing. In the old days you got paid for the year you just had, and if you slumped or broke down, why, the next season either your salary got cut or you did. Now we got some security because it was the owners who were giving 110 percent.

When I became eligible for free agency in '83 they didn't open the office safe and tell me to dig in, but they came up with a lot more than I ever thought of as a kid in LaPorte. I got a three-year deal and Pat and I bought a house in Hinsdale, out west of Chicago.

Everybody wanted Davy Tremayne when he went on the market. He finally left St. Louis and hooked on in New York for something like half the state revenue and his own borough. They say playing there is rough, that the fans, media and front office put plenty of pressure on you, but from a distance I couldn't see that it had much effect on Davy. I figured he could handle it, thinking that his own opinion of himself was so positive that if somebody gave him an unfavorable one he'd just overrule it in his mind.

I got to see Davy look foolish on the field for the first time when he was with New York. We were playing them in the rain at Shea in '83 and Davy tried to stretch a single to right. Alex Ennis picked the ball up near the line and threw to me at second. Davy left his feet in what was supposed to be a head-first slide as the throw came in, but he stuck in the slop about six feet from the base. It gave me such a kick to see him lying there that I drew it out a little; instead of going over and tagging him right away I squatted down and asked, "You comin'?"

He pulled his face out of the ground and laughed. "Don't just let me lie here, dammit," he said, "shoot me."

The crowd acted as happy as I was that Davy had finally done something clumsy. They hooted like hell while I walked over and gave him a little whap on the helmet with my glove.

I spent an evening with Davy shortly after that at this real nice place he had in Manhattan, which he was sharing at the time with a woman who read the news on local television. He told me he'd made some changes on the Never-Land All-Stars.

"I had to give Niff Naffner his unconditional release," he said that night. "I'll never be the Niffer again."

I asked him why and he said, "Niff is the clown who stuck in the mud out at second the other night. After you tagged me out, I got up from there a changed man."

"Who did you change into?"

"Rex 'The Flex' Plexstra," Davy said firmly. "Body-builder. The Flex is too bouncy and buoyant to drive his nose into the dirt six feet from the bag."

He named some other guys he'd added to the team in the years since we'd last talked about it, but I only remember the new manager; Brigadier General "Howling Claude" Reebee, who Davy said had once invented a special kind of airgun pellet for the army called the "Reebee Beebee."

A stranger hearing Davy talk like that might have wondered just how many beebees he was dealing with; Davy showed a more lively interest sometimes in the people he made up than in the actual events of the day. But I took it to be a way of relaxing, getting past some of the pressure. Maybe it was like a secret weapon for him—he had a lot more guys on his team than any other player I knew.

I played in Chicago for ten years altogether, until I was thirty-four. While I did that, moving along and not really noticing the time going by too much, and while Davy was taking the free-agency high road from St. Louis to New York to L.A., Jay Bates took the low road. Or you might say Jay was off on the side streets trying to find his way back to the main thoroughfare.

I didn't see much of Jay, but after a few years kids who'd played for him started coming up to the Chicago club. Jay had made an impression on all of them. Most of them said he knew more baseball than any of the other managers in the chain, but the testimonials pretty much ended there.

All the kids seemed to remember his "I Don't Care If You Hustle" speech. Every new Bates team got this little talk at the beginning of the season, and the versions I heard didn't vary much, so I can put it down here with some confidence. Jay would get the players together in the clubhouse and say this:

"Every other manager you ever have is going to tell you to hustle. They say it's all they can ask, that you stay in the game mentally, and hustle. Well, I don't give a *shit* if you hustle. I don't care if you're out there dreamin' about pussy. I don't care if you take a fuckin' armchair out there and sit in it during the game. They don't list the standings according to hustle. You run out a pop-up? Big deal. Hit the ball over the wall and you can *walk* around the bases jackin' off. If you can beat the other guy *without* hustling, *without* thinking, you can play for me anytime. One thing though: If you ever cost me a *game* because you don't hustle, you can go home and explain to your boyfriends why you don't have an ass anymore."

Jay seemed to like the problem children and the malcontents, as long as they were talented. His prize project was a young black first baseman, Darrell Paris. Darrell told me when he came up that Jay used to work with him for hours on his defense even though Paris called him a lunatic and a racist and a living symbol of four hundred years of white oppression. Darrell said Jay just responded, "What the fuck do you care as long as you make a lot of money?"

Jay was definitely the only manager in the system who was trying to learn Spanish so he could talk to the Latin players. That is not standard, and I was surprised to hear it. Jay's English was pretty confined, and the last thing I would have expected was that he'd be sitting in a room with a book and a cassette so he could become an international man. But I know he put some time into it because years later I heard him carefully picking his way through several sentences of abuse he wanted to pass on to a Dominican pitcher.

He got a couple reprimands from the front office in his first years managing. One time Kramer, the GM, called him in because one of Jay's players had written a letter to the front office saying Jay was a "sociopathic personality." Jay had come up to this young pitcher in the locker room after the kid blew a lead and given him a straight razor, saying, "Here, son. Do the honorable thing." Jay said it was a joke and the other players had laughed. Kramer didn't think it was funny. He said, "I will not have a sociopath running one of our ballclubs." Jay asked what a sociopath was and then said, "Well, shit, if I was one of *those* I woulda cut him myself."

Jay was real careful not to physically attack any of his own players back then, and somehow he lasted long enough to impress the front office with his ability as a manager. Jay's boys came up knowing their baseball; the ones like Paris were smart, aggressive and confident. I think in those years Kramer was usually right on the edge of kissing Jay off, but the truth is that he helped rejuvenate that system. Of course, by the time it really showed at the major league level, Jay and I were both gone.

THEY SAY PROFESSIONAL ATHLETES DIE TWICE, and we do. Our little death, the end of our playing careers, is just as inevitable as the big one. It comes ready or not.

With some guys it's sudden, like a traffic accident; something happens to your body and you can't play anymore. Some die young from a lack of ability, like they had a malnourishment. Most of us just get old and go into a decline. Sometimes we keel over in one season, and spend a brief time on the bench in intensive care before we disappear.

As I got older, I tried little tricks to keep myself in shape—like getting a full night's sleep. I hated the idea of giving up drinking with the boys, but there came a time when I knew if I didn't I'd soon be drinking with a lower economic level of boys. So I gradually cut back on going out at night on the road, and then I stopped altogether. When I was thirty-three I said farewell to beer except for special occasions.

It had its advantages. I didn't miss the hangovers; I didn't miss getting up the next day wanting a grape

Popsicle for breakfast. But I missed some of the silly conversations that players get into when they're out at night. Like arguments about whether the Terminator could kill the Road-Runner, or what your batting average would be if you played on the moon, or how a deaf person can tell when the phone is ringing, and why would he care. Those kinds of subjects don't usually come up at home.

I talked to Davy Tremayne about it once, because he quit drinking entirely around the time I cut back. He said he *did* miss his hangovers: "A man with a bad one," he said, "is fearless. He has nothing to lose. Nothing could make him feel worse than he already does. You don't overthink on the field because you can't think at all. Sometimes things go better if you just cut the crap and swing at the first goddamn pitch to get it over with."

But Davy had become convinced that drinking might interfere with his earning potential somewhere down the line, so he made a vow to himself not to drink again until he'd made twenty-five million dollars.

"Double-digit millions," he once told me, "is as close to security as a guy like me can get. Realistically I can't think about becoming a billionaire. But twenty-five million—that's within my scope. And if I make it, then I'm not saying. I might drink again. You might be driving down the road someday and see me sitting on the corner with a brown bag waving at everybody."

My reasoning was different. Something told me I'd never be one of those people who live on the interest, and I didn't know what I'd be doing after I died as a ballplayer. So I tried to put off my death as long as I could.

I even exercised, which was something I never needed in my twenties. Then I was always the kid. But a ballplayer, after he's thirty-two, the young players start thinking he's Pops, the stage doorman, some marvel of longevity who has to lie down and rest after he reads the paper.

So I did the wind sprints and the calisthenics, and I even did some work with weights. I wouldn't run any distance because I hated it; it was too much work. I'd gotten into ball in the first place so I wouldn't have to work too hard; running miles would have been a contradiction of everything I believed in. You have to draw the line. A man either enjoys what he's doing or he's picking beans; there's no third way about it.

And I held on awhile. I had a little hurrah in my ninth year in Chicago, when we knocked New York out of the divisional race in our last home game. I won it in the eighth, with a home run, only my second of the year, off a lazy curve from Carl Chester. When I got around to the plate I was so unused to doing that "high-ten" thing with the on-deck hitter that I missed the guy's hands completely. That's the happiest I ever saw the Chicago fans while I was playing there. We were out of the race as usual, but they were so thrilled at the rare opportunity to stick it to New York that they just went crazy.

I took Pat and Jamie out that night and Jamie asked me if I was a hero. I said no, doctors and firemen were heroes, but Pat said, "How many times in your life do you think he's going to ask you that?" So I told him, "Well, I'm today's hero." It seemed to satisfy him. It gave him some ammunition to use against the kid at his school who said his dad played for a team that was no good. I was pretty sure I was a hero that night anyway; the doctor and fireman stuff was just what I *thought* I should say.

In my tenth year, though, I was bad. It was my first truly bad season. I hit .231, and it was a struggle to get it up that high. My defense was steady, but plays that used to be easy were harder and plays that used to be hard I couldn't make. I don't know whether it was the old tombstone injury or just natural decline, but I was getting achy and creaky. If I was sitting down and got up I sounded like one of those Latin-band woodblock players.

Toward the end of the year they brought up one of Jay Bates's kids, named Franklin Lee, to try out at short, and I didn't have to be Cosmo the Psychic to see the future when I looked at him. He was twenty-two, fast and thin and all muscle; he *bounded* everywhere. He had a laser arm and a vicious swing and I couldn't have outplayed him in my prime. I felt like an old, arthritic family cocker spaniel who looks up and sees the head of the house bring home a six-month-old Doberman. I could snarl all I wanted but I was still going to have to get out of the way.

Over the winter Kramer, the GM, looked at his short-stop options. Franklin Lee was fresh bread and I was day-old; he could keep me until I got moldy, throw me out, or give me to the poor and starving. Kramer did the last thing—he traded me in spring training across town to Chicago's American League entry, one of the worst teams in baseball.

When I made my last tour of the locker room Alex Ennis wouldn't even say goodbye, since I wasn't leaving town. He told me to keep an eye on his house during the summer.

It felt funny. I approved the trade because I had a better chance of playing regularly if I left, but I'd never been in another organization before. It had always been the other guys who came and went, not me. I'd gotten to feeling I'd always be in the same clubhouse and now I wasn't. Somehow getting traded brought it home to me that I really was going to die someday.

I didn't sparkle on the South Side, and I don't have many happy memories of the league that gave me the opportunity to bat ninth for the first time in my career. The pitchers and hitters were strangers to me. In the NL I could almost *feel* where the ball was going to be hit when I was at short, but here I was always reacting, I couldn't anticipate. The Sox played me long enough to convince themselves I wasn't the answer to their prayers; at the end of the season they wished me luck and joy and said I could come to spring training as a nonroster player.

I eventually signed a one-year deal in Philadelphia, in my old league, back where I'd played my first game. I was a utilityman for them for a season and then I was through.

But I finally got to be in a pennant race. We took New York and Pittsburgh right down to the wire that year and we won the damn thing, we won the division.

I mostly rode the pine in Philly, but I did get into some big ballgames in September, when the pressure was on and guys were chewing their spit. I'd always wondered how I'd do in that spot. I've never seen a player completely freeze with the season on the line, to where he couldn't function at all, but I've seen hitters strangle the bat handle and yank their heads on the swing, trying to hit the ball to Jupiter. And I've seen pitchers grab a bunt and whirl around like they were at the Little Big Horn, waiting too long to throw and then throwing anyway, past everybody. It can get scary out there when you're making history.

Fortunately, the one thing Philly counted on me to do was the one thing I still *could* do—catch the ball. I must be a grounder billionaire. I've seen a lot of hops. There wasn't a ball that came to me in that pennant race that I hadn't seen before. And I found out something good about that pressure—it takes away pain. My adrenaline would get going so good in the late innings that my knees didn't hurt until afterward.

I made the plays. I didn't have many to make, but they were important and I made them.

And then I was done. I sat on the bench in the postseason and soaked up the atmosphere while we won the playoffs and lost the Series in six to Detroit. I batted twice and grounded out both times, and fielded 1.000 with a putout and three assists.

I got a ring and died happy.

It takes some getting used to, that "Where did everybody go?" feeling. In fact, I didn't *get* used to it. I got cut loose two years ago, and at thirty-seven I was so accustomed to all the people—teammates, opponents, reporters, fans—being around me and watching what I did that I felt lost when it stopped. It was *quiet* that fall.

My oldest job option was out. Dad had gotten tired of fending off those little convenience stores that took over the country while I was playing ball, and he closed up shop, so we would never be Tyke & Son. He and Mom were comfortable in LaPorte and willing to have us there any time and all, but Pat and I wanted to stay in Chicago and I wanted to stay in baseball.

I'd thought of asking Lou Haddix for a coaching job on my old club—he'd been the manager the last couple years—but he got sacked about when I did. Then I half-expected to hear from Jay Bates.

I thought Jay would get to manage in Chicago. He'd been working his way up while I was working my way out; the last three years he'd managed at Wichita and done well. He knew all the players in the organization and it seemed logical to give him a shot at the top.

But he didn't get it. I heard from some guys associated with the team that he offended Kramer by *demanding* the job after Haddix's firing. Apparently it irritated Jay that they were even interviewing other people, so he came on too strong in his own talk with Kramer. They wound up hiring a coach from Detroit who was supposed to be a genius because they'd won last year. Jay went back to Kansas a little yanked off.

The night sky in Wichita must have really lit up when Jay heard that Davy Tremayne had been named player-manager in St. Louis. Davy represented the old glory days to the people down there; they hadn't won since he started his free-agent wanderings, so when his lease expired in Los Angeles they brought him back. Nobody really knew if he could manage, but he could still play some and figured to improve attendance.

I sent out feelers to every team in the Midwest but

Davy gave me my only nibble. He called up in November and said, "I've got to stick with a couple of these coaches until we get rolling and then I'm gonna trash 'em. If you're still available when they go maybe we can do business. You've got a great coach's name, Charlie; you'll land on your feet."

I would've preferred a little confidence in my baseball sense rather than in my name. I thought Davy might limit himself as a manager if he only wanted to hire people who sounded good when you called them.

"Davy, do you just read the first two words on the resume?"

"Oh, you're qualified, too, Charlie," he said. "I'd never take anybody who wasn't qualified. But people live up to their names. Mickey Mantle hit like Mickey Mantle and Wayne Terwilliger hit like Wayne Terwilliger."

"Well, you better not manage like Brigadier General Howling Claude Reebee or you'll never make twenty-five million."

"You don't make it managing anyway," he said. "Investments, Charlie. The aggressively handled portfolio."

I had one other employment opportunity and I took it, but I underestimated its difficulty.

I'd heard a lot of baseball broadcasts in my life, and I always thought I'd make a good announcer. I found out later that everybody thinks that; baseball announcing is just one of those jobs we all think we can do, like kicking field goals. It seems easy to any player or fan—you just say what's going on. And the players think they're smarter about the game than the regular announcers, anyway. I know I did.

During my playing days in Chicago I'd been up in the booth a couple times when I was on the DL and they let me do play-by-play for an inning or so. I had a good time and they liked me, so I talked to the station people that winter and did one of those demos. They thought it was good enough to try me out doing color with the radio guy, Maury Hairston.

I was proud of myself. This *was* landing on my feet. Pat was delighted because I wouldn't be on the road any more than I'd ever been—it would be just like playing, only I could do it even if I got old and fat.

I look back now and wonder what I was thinking of. I spent seventeen years preparing to be a major league player and four months preparing to be a major league broadcaster.

Jamie loves these teenager movies where the kid at school always gets picked on by bullies, but secretly all his life he's wanted to be checker champion of East Lynne, New Jersey, and they show him training with his kindly old checker coach and doing chin-ups and running to improve his stamina for the big match, when he triple-jumps the bully kid in the city finals. Those movies always seem corny to me, but they do point up the importance of extensive preparation. When it came time for me to hit the airwaves I was under-rehearsed.

My biggest attribute as an announcer, I think, was my appearance—I looked all right and dressed well, which doesn't matter a hell of a lot in radio.

It turned out that without my knowledge I'd acquired a number of speech habits that can wear the listener down. I had the "wells" and the "y'knows" and the "really incredibles" pretty bad. There isn't much inside baseball information in the sentence, "Well, y'know, Maury, when you think about it, that play Johnson made was really, y'know, incredible."

It also was called to my attention that every time Hairston made a comment I responded, "You got *that* right, Maury." I was very agreeable. A guy came up to me in a restaurant one night and *begged* me just once to say, "That's true, Maury," or even "Bullshit, Maury"—anything but "You got *that* right" every goddamn time.

Hairston tried to help me by going over my habits and winnowing out the meaningless words, but there were so *many*. Once I knew about them I got worse. Then I'd say things like, "Well, y'know, that was really—oh." Sometimes I got afraid to talk at all and just froze up and watched the game for an inning or so while Maury answered all his own questions.

One night in Pittsburgh a guy dropped an easy fly and Maury asked me what happened to him. I was determined not to say the same old thing so I blurted out, "He should've caught it in his jock." Maury paused for a second and said, "You got *that* right, Charlie."

I got a little better as the year went on. Pat worked with me at home. I gave her one of those little clickers and told her to click it every time I said "y'know" or "really incredible." When she got tired of being the percussion section Jamie was glad to take over.

At the end of the year Maury told me I was going to be a good announcer someday, and our employers told me I was going to have to do it elsewhere. The demand for

Charlie Tyke in the Chicago baseball market had been, y'know, satisfied.

By fall my immediate options had narrowed down to staying home and watching TV. I think watching it as much as I did must have made me a little deranged. I got thinking I could be an actor. Seeing all the ex-athletes on TV gave me an idea—if you're an actor, I figured, they write all your words down for you and all you have to do is remember.

I was about to call up the light beer people to get started when the phone rang one night and Jay Bates said, "I just signed to manage the Rush. You want a job?"

By February I was in California, working for Jay and teaching Bates-ball.

9

SUNSET BOONE MOVIES WERE ALWAYS AMONG
my favorites when I was a kid; one of the comics
my mother got me the day I smashed my knee was a
Sunset Boone. I was one of his little pardners. Last
winter I became his little pardner again, because he was
the owner of the California Rush.

Ever since around 1958 the baseball people have been
convinced that California is the place they oughta be, and
when the major leagues expanded again last year they
realigned all the divisions and old Sunset got a franchise in
Santa Rita, south of Los Angeles. The Rush was put in a
division that included San Diego, L.A., San Francisco,
Chicago, St. Louis and Houston. And the name for the
team was a good one because it had to be put together in
a hurry.

Sunset was a movie star with brains who had invested
wisely, but he didn't have a baseball background, so he
hired the old Toronto GM, Ralph Jessup, to organize his
club. Jessup told him the best manager available to get a
team winning in a hurry was probably Jay Bates, as long
as you could stand him. And when Jay interviewed he

must have turned on his best approximation of charm, because Sunset liked him.

All the other candidates Boone and Jessup talked to said things like, "I won't lie to you, Sunset; it takes time to build a winner." Jay said, "I'll find twenty-four guys who can play." Sunset loved that kind of talk. He thought Jay was quick on the draw.

I had my share of doubts about working for Jay. After he called with the offer I remember comparing him in my mind with what I knew of historically rough bosses, like Hitler and Al Capone, and finding some similarities. It was an exciting prospect, being there at the beginning when a new team was built, but there was no point in looking for a house in California if I took the job. Coaches don't generally stay in one place very long, and *Jay's* coaches figured to be even more temporary than the usual run.

Pat had never met Jay, but I'd told her a little about him, and she was dubious about the whole thing.

"He sounds like an asshole," she said when we discussed it.

I thought it over. "I guess if you had to sum him up," I nodded. "But he knows his baseball and he works hard. And I can't be choosy. Unless I try acting."

"I think," she said, "that whatever talent you have as an actor will probably keep."

We decided I'd give it a shot. Pat stayed home and Jamie stayed in school in Hinsdale. Pat was freelancing for papers and magazines in Chicago by then; she'd started with a piece about being married to a ballplayer, called "Mrs. Hero, Mrs. Goat," and then she moved on to other stories of people around town, so it was logical for her to stay for now. I flew out to California and Jay picked me up at John Wayne Airport.

Jay was happy. Oh, he was fired up. He was punching the air walking to the car.

"I *made* it," he said. "I'm here. They'll have to kill me to get me outta here now. Where's Fred Brice? Huh? Where's those guys on that team in Chicago now? I'm here and they're gone, that's where they are. They fell off the ladder."

"Well, you earned it, Jay," I said. "You did the years you had to do."

"I did one too many. Kramer shoulda hired me last season, the prick. You know what I did when they hired me? I went to Gary. First time I been home in twelve years. They interviewed me in the goddamn paper. There's guys back there working in the mills shitting *blood* because I made it. They can't fuckin' stand it. I'm tellin' ya, man, it's a riot.

"This is just the start, y'know. It's one thing to show up the losers in Gary and another to feed it to the big boys up here. We gotta make a ballclub here. Twenty-four maniacs, that's what we need. Just like me. You think I'm a maniac, don't ya?"

"Oh, I don't know."

"Well, I'm not. I hold myself in all the time."

Meeting Sunset Boone was a big moment for me. The Old Wrangler. I liked him best in that film where he played Arthur Law, the drifter who became a peace officer; they called him Marshal Law, and his friends called him Marshal Art. Of course that was years ago;

nowadays Sunset mostly rides the phone, making deals
and bringing people to their knees with his shrewd business tactics and so on.

That afternoon Jay brought me into Sunset's big office
in about the only tall building they have in Santa Rita,
because of earthquakes, I guess. He was shorter than I
thought he'd be, and old, of course, and bald, and he
wore a suit. Other than that he was just like in the
movies. He shook hands with me across his desk when
Jay introduced us.

"I was one of your little pardners, Mr. Boone," I said.

"Damn right you were," he said. "How you feel about
bein' pardners again?"

"Great!" I said. I was starstruck.

"Hope you boys are as good as you're s'posed to be,"
he said. "Folks out here like winners, there's lots of
winners out here. Lots of competition for the entertain-
ment dollar. Folks can get here from L.A., and they can
get here from the beach towns. They'll come if you put
on a good show and they'll find twenty other things to do
every day if you don't."

"They'll come to see this club, sir," said Jay. Sunset
and I were both a little shocked at that "sir."

"It's 'Sunset,' son," said the Old Wrangler. "Don't be
shy around me. Jessup told me you were a real nails-for-
breakfast fella. Walk your own trail and be your own man
and don't ever put me on hold." He laughed. "Now, boys,
I'm kickin' y'all outta here. Got some calls to make. Get
together with Jessup and pick me out some ballplayers."

"I like *him* a lot better than those happy horseshit
movies he made," Jay said as we left.

Jessup was a little less chummy when we met him in his office at the ballpark. He was a heavy man in his late fifties with sad brown eyes; he always looked like he was sorry he'd let you in.

He told Jay, "I went out on a limb picking you. Kramer in Chicago told me you're quite a dose. Don't second-guess me in the papers and don't hand any razors to the players. I know what you said to Sunset about winning this year and that's nice, but you're talking to a baseball man now. I want us competitive in four years. If you can keep on an even keel you'll be here when that happens."

I thought, great. Excellent. That gives us some margin, that's realistic.

Jay said, "Get me the players I want and we'll be over .500 the first year or you can fire my ass."

Expansion teams pick their players out of a pool of guys made available by the other existing clubs, and the reason most of these fellas are available is because they aren't any good. That's why expansion teams usually stink up the league for their first few years.

You can go two ways when you're drafting for a new team; you can try to win some games quick by picking up veterans who may have a year left in them, or you can take the long-haul approach and go with unproven kids. Jay and Jessup agreed they'd take the kids in the draft, but Jay planned on winning early anyway, which of course is considered to be impossible.

The training camp at Palm Springs was a carnival. Besides the guys Jay and Jessup drafted out of other organizations we had all kinds of invitees and walk-ons from colleges and bar leagues and God knows where else. Jay was so sure he could figure a kid's chances on sight that he wasn't overwhelmed by a camp with a hundred guys in it, but I felt surrounded.

I saw more collisions in the first few days of that camp than I've ever seen anywhere. I think Jay put all those kids in the outfield just so they'd run into each other and he could keep the three that got up. We had second basemen and shortstops who both went to cover on the steal and smashed themselves; catchers and first basemen stepping on each other under foul pops; outfielders tottering around in circles holding their heads while the ball rolled to the wall. Sunset Boone came to camp one day and watched our kids demolishing themselves and said to Jay, "We oughta film this team in Collide-O-Scope."

Jay liked it. He liked the guys who kept running balls-out even after they'd crashed a time or two, and cut the ones who shied away.

And out of all this mess Jay started spotting guys he liked. He liked Joe Surface, a third baseman who'd never made it in the Atlanta organization. Surface took a bad hop in the mouth one day and still threw the batter out, which made him a Jay Bates third baseman. He liked Marty Miranda at shortstop because Marty had some pop in his bat and never seemed to say anything except "Bueno." His favorite outfielder was a kid named John Turk, who was short but real sturdy, built kind of like a street-corner mailbox. When *he* ran into people in the outfield he was unaware of it.

Second base went to Tony Biela, from the San Francisco scrap heap. Tony was already thirty-four but Jay wanted him out there because he needed at least one guy who knew what he was doing.

Angelo Fanzone got the job in right field even though he struck out half the time because he was massive, a crusher good for thirty homers or more if he ever learned to open his eyes when he swung. What Davy Tremayne would have called a Niff Naffner type.

Our fastest man by far was the center fielder, J. W. Shain, a twenty-two-year-old black kid who thought he could hit better than he really could. He also thought he was prettier than paradise. J.W. was blessed with confidence. He insisted he had "super-speed" and could move faster than the eye could see. He was always racing up behind people when they weren't looking and asking them how they thought he got there.

Jay liked Tom Gonder at catcher because he fit the "maniac" qualifications. He was aggressive and fearless but tough to keep in one piece.

Young guys are capable of injuring themselves in ways an old guy isn't; an old guy just wouldn't think of the ways these kids hurt themselves. Gonder missed a big chunk of spring training because he fell off Joe Surface's car and then Surface hit him with it.

Gonder and Surface were out drinking one night and concluded at about 4:00 A.M. that it would be a good idea to drive down one of the quieter Palm Springs roads with Gonder on the hood. This was all Gonder's idea, by the way. He told Surface he wanted some air.

So they're cruising down Sonny Bono Lane or something with Gonder reclining on the front of Surface's ancient El Dorado, and Gonder doesn't know he can't brace his foot against the hood ornament because it's on a spring and bends over at the first pressure. So when Surface starts to brake at an intersection, Gonder puts his foot on the ornament and it bends over and Gonder slides right off the hood in front of the car and it knocks him down on his face and scrapes off his profile before Surface can stop it completely.

Gonder wasn't completely ruined except for his looks, which hadn't been alluring to begin with. After the accident he could make a grown man scream. He wanted to sue Surface or the El Dorado people for not telling the world their hood ornaments were unstable, but the cops told him he didn't have much of a case because the car was designed to have the passengers ride on the inside. When Gonder got out of the hospital the players called him "Broadway," "Asphalt" and "Scrape-Face" and told him he had to wear his mask at all times.

Now this team was a cast of might-bes and could-have-beens for the most part, but they all shared an attitude—they were all pretty belligerent and they all thought they were better than other people thought they were. What Jay needed to give them some legitimacy was a guy who really *was* acknowledged to be good; for first base he wanted Jessup to get Darrell Paris, from Chicago.

Darrell was in the last year of a big contract there and had fallen out with management over his attitude. They thought he was moody and selfish and a "cancer on the team" and all that stuff. Darrell didn't like what they were saying about him and suggested that Kramer should "give him some head for Christmas," so he was available. Jay, of course, didn't care if Darrell was a cancer. He talked Jessup into rounding up every prospect we had left over, some of whom were supposed to be good, and packaging five of them in a trade with Chicago to get Darrell for one year. Jessup didn't think it was a smart long-term move, but he agreed that Paris would bring some people to the park. We needed at least one honest-to-God, diamond-studded star, and Jessup made the deal and we got Darrell.

Now Jay had eight men to go out on the field and all he needed was somebody to pitch, which was where his one technical weakness was. Jay didn't know quite what to say to pitchers. They're a different breed, and require different handling.

Pitching successfully is tricky; if you think about it long enough it becomes impossible. The only advice Jay had picked up to give to his pitchers was "Throw strikes but don't give 'em anything good to hit," which *is* the key to pitching, but pitchers don't really need to be told that. They already know. It's like telling a race-car driver to go fast but don't crash.

Jay left the handling of the staff to Red McDevitt, the pitching coach. Red settled on a cross-section of America that included Ron Amalfimatanio and Fabian Koonce, and Fabian, of course, turned out to be the eye of the cyclone in the Last Game.

From a personal standpoint, it was a lively bunch. Most of these guys were so happy to be getting a chance to play that it made them bouncy. We had a dynamic clubhouse, what with Tony Biela juggling and J. W. Shain darting around and Angelo Fanzone doing his karate "kata" and José Ochoa, the utility infielder, doing his impressions. There's something extra entertaining about hearing a Latin who can barely speak English doing an impression of Jack Nicholson. Ochoa was also fun to watch when he mimicked Jay Bates ("You got to *heet* de fuckeen ball, chackoff!").

But from a baseball standpoint it wasn't as promising. We got beat a lot in the exhibition games, and the media experts all said we were going to get beat a lot in the regular season too. Expectations were low.

At the end of camp Sunset Boone threw a party for the players in a restaurant in Palm Springs. The day of the party I couldn't get to Jay at all; he was holed up in his office and wouldn't come out or let anybody in. He said he was working on something. I suspected it was his little speech for the party.

The spring was Jay's first real experience talking to a lot of people. Up till that point in his career nobody'd been too interested in what he had to say, but now, as a manager in the bigs, he was getting approached by reporters and asked his opinion about things. He didn't have to censor himself with the newspapermen, but he was uncomfortable talking to broadcasters and the general public because he couldn't express himself very well without full use of his vocabulary.

At the party that night, after we all ate our dinners, Sunset Boone got up and made a speech about how Opening Day was the first step on a long trail and a man's not beat till he's pushing up the daisies. Then Jay got up. He had figured out that this wasn't the time for his "I

Don't Care If You Hustle" speech, and I was curious to hear what he'd say. There were a few people from the press there and this was in the nature of public speaking.

Jay was nervous. He wasn't a drinking man but he probably could have used a couple that evening. He cleared his throat and looked kind of like he had years ago when he went up to LuAnn in the Monmouth bar. Then he pulled a raggedy piece of paper from his coat pocket and read from it:

"Chicago won't win 'cause their pitching is bad; L.A. can't score in the clutch/Houston's too old and Frisco's too slow, and nobody likes San Diego too much/Everyone thinks that we'll finish last, and St. Louis will win 'cause they hit/But everybody's been wrong at times in the past, and I think they're all full of shit."

Now he didn't read it too well, he got the rhythm all cockeyed, but I can state that that little speech was successful. Darrell Paris about died laughing and so did I—not so much because of the *quality* of it as the idea that Jay had actually stood up and read a poem. We couldn't believe it. This was a side of Jay that nobody had seen before.

I asked him later how long it took him to write it and he said two days. He said he got the ending right away and worked backward.

10

THIS WAS OUR OPENING DAY LINEUP:

> J. W. Shain, CF
> Tony Biela, 2B
> Darrell Paris, 1B
> John Turk, LF
> Angelo Fanzone, RF
> Joe Surface, 3B
> Tom Gonder, C
> Marty Miranda, SS
> Ron Amalfimatanio, P

I think the sportswriters were hoping Ron Amalfimatanio wouldn't make it; at least the headline writers were. But Jay and the pitching coach, McDevitt, had him penciled in as the staff horse. He threw hard and they thought he could give us 250 innings. So did he. Top to bottom our lineup had more confidence and less apparent reason for it than any other team in the league.

We opened at home, against Chicago, and had a nice crowd of the curious to start out the season. Sunset

Boone threw out the first ball, and the organist played his old theme song, "Sleepin' 'Neath the Stars Is Good Enough for Me."

I would've liked to have played. I missed it. But at least I was going to be on the field, in uniform, in the third-base coach's box. And who knew? If we turned out to be as bad as people said we would, I might be reactivated. Like all old ballplayers I was always going around saying, "Well, I *know* I could do better than *him.*"

It was a pretty night, like they mostly are in Southern California, and everybody was bright-eyed and unblemished. Nobody'd made an out yet, nobody'd made an error, anything was possible.

We were three runs down before any of the fans could order a beer. Amalfimatanio was hyper and walked a couple guys, then he gave up a homer. Jay didn't move a muscle on the bench. McDevitt said, "You want me to go out there?" Jay said, "Nahh. Let's see what he's got in him."

And that was the major managerial decision of the night. Ron got mad and settled down and only gave up one run the rest of the way. Darrell Paris hit one out in the fourth and another in the sixth and we went into the ninth with a 5–4 lead.

The game ended on a weird play. Chicago had a guy on first with two out and there was a grounder to third. Surface grabbed it and threw toward second for the force but let go too soon and it went off Biela's glove into short right field. The ball started rolling along in no man's land while the Chicago runner went to third, rounded it and started for home with the tying run.

Darrell Paris finally chased the ball down in right but he was running away from home and had no chance to get the runner, so he flipped it underhand to Angelo Fanzone, who was coming in from right, and Fanzone threw the guy out at the plate. If you were scoring that play it went 5-4-3-9-2.

The crowd ate it up and so did Jay, who said he'd taught Darrell that play in the minors. Darrell said bullshit, he just had great instincts. Sunset said in an interview after the game, "Folks, if you want to see baseball the way it oughta be played, come back tomorrow and we'll try doin' it that way." A reporter in an L.A. paper wrote, "Presumably the Rush will win the division if Darrell Paris, as projected, hits 324 home runs."

Jay'd been hoping for a fast start at home and he got one. Paris carried us for the first three weeks; he had nine homers in April and led the league in everything. By the end of the month we were 11–7 and then everybody started pitching around him.

Our respectable start was a cute story for the papers, but nobody expected us to keep it up. The division heavyweight was still St. Louis, and Davy Tremayne's club went 13–5 in the first month.

I didn't get much rest after Opening Day. Jay wanted me around or available all the time, even after we left the park, because he said he could talk to me easier than anybody else. I don't think he slept at all, or if he did it was all short naps. He'd call me up in the middle of the night to discuss whether we should put a shift on against the L.A. first baseman or arrange a call-girl service for the players on the road so they wouldn't waste energy "hunting pussy."

Jay himself didn't go out much, and I didn't see him with women. It took me until May to find out he'd been married while he was managing in the minors; I'd missed the whole thing. It didn't last very long. The girl was a waitress in Wichita and Jay said the marriage broke up because she drank too much and wouldn't leave him alone.

I got lonely for Pat and Jamie and they came out to Santa Rita for Jamie's Easter school break. That was the first time they'd ever met Jay.

Jay liked to pick me up at my apartment in the morning and drive me to the park so he could talk over any ideas he had in the car on the way. He came over the morning after Pat and Jamie arrived and I introduced everybody.

"Hi, kid," said Jay to Jamie. "You a baseball fan?"

"Sure," said Jamie.

"Who's your favorite team?"

"Chicago."

"What about the Rush?"

"Dad says they're playing over their heads."

Jay looked at me. "What the hell kind of attitude is that?"

"I was quoting the papers, Jay," I said. Then I asked Pat, "Haven't you taught this kid to check his sources?"

Pat offered her hand to Jay and said, "Charlie says you're the perfect manager for a team of overachievers."

Jay shook hands with her, muttering, "The writers never know a goddamn thing. All newspaper writers know how to do is shovel it. You out here for a while?"

"No, I have to get back home at the end of the week and do some shoveling," said Pat.

In the car on the way to the park Jay got to screaming at a guy who cut him off on the freeway and I said, "You see life as pretty much of a war, don't ya, Jay?"

"What do *you* think it is, a bowling alley?"

"Just people trying to get by, I guess."

"Maybe in Mayberry, but not where I come from. To get *by*, you got to get by the *other* guy tryin' to get by. There's only room for one at the front. How many teams are gonna be champ at the end of the year? One. You played ten years in Chicago, spinnin' your wheels on a team that was satisfied to lose. Got comfortable, gained fifteen pounds, lost your speed. You could turn into another one of these fat puppies on the road who don't know they're nothin'. I weigh what I weighed at Monmouth. If you don't stay hungry you'll never get full." He leaned on the horn and mumbled to the driver ahead, "This is the fast lane, asshole." At least I *assume* he was talking to the driver ahead.

Fabian Koonce is notorious now, but even at the beginning of the season he stood out for me. He was a sight—a heavyset farm boy with goggly glasses. He looked like Woody Allen, only huge. He came from Quincy, Illinois, right across the river from my home town, and he was so big that McDevitt called him "Baby Huey" after the old comic book character. He had hefty bones and some fat on him, and he had real white skin except for his neck and arms, like farmers often do. You'd think

106

a kid that large would throw hard, but he didn't; he had a below-average fastball and even slower breaking stuff, with little wrinkles in it. The only thing he really had going for him was control; he could put the ball where he wanted.

Fabian didn't talk much, and when he did he used what you might call country sayings, only I don't know what country they were from. I couldn't understand what he meant half the time and I grew up fifteen miles away from him.

One time he came back to the bench from striking out on a terrible pitch, over his head, and Jay asked him what he was doing up there. Koonce shook his head and said, "Skip, I was fishin' for crows in the wind." Jay looked at me blankly and I said, "I guess he means he was doing something foolish." I would imagine it's foolish to fish for crows in the wind.

We closed out camp with ten pitchers and Koonce was one of them, but Jay wasn't sure about him. He had him in the bullpen in early May, when we went east to St. Louis for our first series with the favorites. It was the first time Jay Bates and Davy Tremayne had met in years.

On the night of the series opener, just before the game, Davy walked to our dugout and came over to where Jay and I were sitting. He was a little heavier than he'd been in his prime but he still looked like the star of the show. He started talking to us like he was picking up a conversation that started yesterday.

"Got a lad on my club, George Washington, can't be-lieve I was ever a kid and played in the minors with you two," he said easily. " 'Course George is a real here-and-now type thinker, doesn't care much for history. He doesn't even know he's named after anybody in particular." Davy shook hands with me and decided not to give a hand to Jay, who was chewing gum and staring out at the field. "I told him Jay here about cut my bowels out at second back in the dead-ball days. Who'da thought back then we'd be doin' this now, huh?"

"Smith's been winnin' for ya, hasn't he?" I said.

Davy looked over his shoulder to where Lefty Smith, his new free agent, was warming up down the left-field line.

"He's been sharp," Davy admitted. "I can't get behind that nickname of his, though. Lefty Smith. The players call him 'Lefty' or 'Smitty.' " Davy shook his head. "I call him 'Colorful Nickname' Smith." He gazed at Jay, who was still steadfastly looking at nothing. "Well . . . I got responsibilities now, can't stand around lettin' Jay talk my ear off all night. Put a lid on it, Jay."

Davy headed back to his own dugout and I said to Jay, "Couldn't you place him?"

Jay looked at me and said, "You ain't paid to buddy up to him."

"I shook his hand, Jay, I didn't kiss it."

Jay sent me out with the lineup card to meet Davy and the umpires before the game started. He really didn't have anything to say to Davy at that point. To Jay, for whom existence was a series of paybacks, Davy still held all the cards and there was nothing to talk about until the personal score between them wasn't so lopsided.

This game was the first opportunity Jay had gotten to wipe a millimeter off Davy's smile, and Jay wanted it bad. Payback didn't start on this evening, though. Jay got thrown out of his first game of the year—after it was over.

Seems like expansion teams get involved in more odd plays than the regular teams. You spend all this time in spring training drilling on the fundamentals and then the game is on the line and something happens that simply hasn't been gone over.

Fabian Koonce was on in relief in the ninth and the score was tied. St. Louis had Washington, the kid Tremayne had mentioned, on second with one out. Koonce threw a pretty good sinker on two and two and the hitter swung and, we thought, foul-tipped it into the dirt. But the ump signaled strike three, which would have been fine except the ball bounced past Gonder to the screen. Washington, the runner, went to third, rounded it and headed home. Gonder ran back and got the ball and Koonce came in to cover. The ball got to Koonce before Washington did and Fabian put his glove down on the plate for the tag, which would have been fine, too, except Washington didn't slide. He kind of hopped over Koonce's glove and the ump signaled safe and the game was over.

Jay was steamed. I was a little mad myself, and I ran out there too, but I never got much of a word in. Jay was all *over* Art Lemon, the plate ump.

"First off, the ball was foul!" said Jay.

"No, it wasn't, the guy missed it," said Lemon.

"And *second* off, Washington was out!"

"No, he wasn't."

"Koonce had his glove on the plate!"

"The guy stepped over it, Jay," said Lemon.

"Then he missed the plate!"

"No, he got a little piece with his heel."

"How the fuck could he have got a piece with his heel? Koonce, put your glove on the plate."

"Okay, skip," said Koonce, and did.

"Look at that!" screamed Jay. "Where's the guy gonna step? He's got it covered!"

"He didn't do it like that before, there was a little piece showing."

"He had to step on the fuckin' glove! Look at the fuckin' glove, for crissakes, it's got a lace ripped out!"

Then Koonce said, "It was like that before, skip."

Jay stared at Fabian like he was the Masked Asshole.

"What happened, Jay," said Lemon, "is your pitcher assumed the other guy was going to slide and he didn't, he stepped over his glove."

"And *missed the plate!*" yelled Jay.

"Nope, he got a sliver of it."

"A sliver? A *sliver?* Lemon, you fuckin' homer, he missed the plate!"

"*You're outta here!*" yelled Lemon, and threw his thumb down like he was spiking a football. The crowd loved it.

No ump will put up with being called a "homer," which is an ump who lets the crowd's preference influence his decisions. Jay kept after Lemon for a few more minutes but everybody was packing up to leave and there wasn't much more to be said.

What made Jay madder than anything else besides losing to Tremayne was that Koonce had made that remark about the lace on his glove. He didn't think that had been the moment for Koonce to be a Boy Scout. I talked to the kid in the clubhouse afterward and suggested he give Jay some leeway for a while.

"You're not under oath out there, y'know," I told him.

"Well, that lace was already tore. If I'da said it was tore on that play I'da been lyin', and a Koonce don't lie."

I looked at him. "Does a Koonce shut up?"

Koonce looked at the floor. "He ken."

"Well, in the future when Jay's out there and says it happened *this* way, don't say it happened *that* way. He doesn't require your testimony."

"Think I oughta apologize to him?" Koonce asked.

"Not tonight. Not tonight. Just stay in the back of the bus."

Jay was dismantling his office when I went in to see him.

" 'It was like that before, skip,' " he sang through his nose. "What a fuckin' dummy. What a gogglehead. That's a ballplayer? That's a fuckin' 4-H Future Farmer of America."

"I talked to him," I said.

"*Talked* to him! Bring him in here, *I'll* talk to him. I'll let some *air* out of him."

"Maybe you oughta wait. He already knows he did wrong."

"He might forget. Bring him in."

I went and found Koonce and brought him in. He was still in his jock. He looked like a giant baby with glasses. Jay was leaning back against the front of his desk with his arms folded.

"Koonce," said Jay, "what do you say when you throw a ball and the ump calls it a strike?"

Koonce looked bewildered for a second and then said, "Nothin'."

"What do you say when you're out and the ump calls you safe?"

Koonce looked miserable. "Nothin'," he said.

"Then why, when I say you got a lace torn off your glove on a play at the plate, do you say, 'It was like that before'?"

Koonce swallowed and shook his head. "I don't know. I guess I'm just a tick on a turd."

Jay looked at me. "What the hell does *that* mean?"

I shrugged. "I guess it means he's misguided."

"It better mean he's *stupid*," said Jay, looking Koonce up and down. Jay didn't like to be what he called "counterdicted," and he said, "Don't ever counterdict me again, Koonce."

"Okay, skip." Koonce started out.

"Hey, Koonce," said Jay. Fabian stopped at the door and looked back. "There's a fly on your ear."

Koonce brushed at his ear. "No, there ain't," he said.

"Kid, what did I just tell you?"

"There's a fly on my ear."

"Before that."

Koonce thought about it. "Don't counterdict you."

"Okay. There's a fly on your ear."

Koonce stroked his ear a little, looking puzzled. "I don't feel it," he said. I closed my eyes for a second to rub the lids.

"The point I'm tryin' to make, kid," said Jay, "is that if I say something is so, as far as you're concerned it's so.

And I say there's a fuckin' *fly* on your *ear,* and if you don't swat it I'll swat it myself."

Koonce finally got it and gave himself a whack on the side of the head.

Jay said, "You missed it. But keep trying. Try all night if you have to."

Koonce looked down at the floor again and then turned and left. Jay stared at the office door and said, "I shoulda told him it was on his dick."

MOST MANAGERS HAVE A REVOLVING-DOOR doghouse. A player screws up and goes in, but next day he's back out and no hard feelings. These managers get mad fast and get over it fast. It's probably the best way to handle things over the course of a season.

Jay's doghouse, though, was shy on exits. When Fabian Koonce went in, he stayed in. I had thought after Jay's conversation with him in his office that it was old business, but I should have known better. A Koonce don't lie; a Bates don't forget.

Fabian's run-in with Jay kicked off a team slump that lasted through May. Paris wasn't seeing anything good to hit and nobody else was hitting it when they saw it. We got eaten up by everybody on a long road trip and when we got home late in the month we were in fifth place, six games under .500.

Koonce wasn't the only culprit, but he seemed to represent losing to Jay, somehow. Jay now had it in his head that Fabian was an idiot and he treated him accordingly. We had a complicated system of signs for our hitters, but when Koonce was up, Jay would have me walk down from the third-base box and give the sign right in his ear. "Huey don't understand strategy," Jay said to everybody.

At first during the slump, Jay tried to be encouraging, telling the players they could boost themselves back up, but after a while he started reverting to his actual personality. When we came home and lost a TV Game of the Week to L.A., something like 13–2, Jay sat on the bench like the Human Torch all through the contest and addressed most of his remarks to himself. It was the first time the TV-viewing nation had seen the Rush. Not much of a show. The L.A. batters did laps around the bases, similar to a track relay. When we got way behind, Jay had McDevitt bring Koonce in, and he got shelled worse than the first pitchers. He didn't walk anybody though, which was more than our other guys could say.

Jay came to see Koonce as a symbol of hard times, sort of a walking slump, but he wasn't really that bad. Or rather, you could see that someday he might be good. He just had to put the ball *exactly* where he wanted it; if he was slightly off he got lit up. The rest of us rooted for him a little extra because we liked him.

Originally I think *I* liked him because he was from my area of the world; he swam in the same river I did. I wanted to help him figure out where the hotel was and how much to tip the cabbie. There aren't too many legitimate rubes in baseball anymore; everybody is at least a little sophisticated. There are more college boys, and even the ones without much education have seen enough television to know there are such things as suits and ties and credit cards and tall buildings. But Fabe was pretty pure country. His mail consisted of letters from home about how his daddy was having trouble with the farm machinery; McDevitt called them "John Deere letters."

J. W. Shain enjoyed Fabian. Shain was a kid from Oakland who'd seen several sights growing up, and running into Koonce, who hadn't seen anything but Quincy, delighted him. He loved to hear Fabian talk. Because Koonce threw slow, and ran slow, and talked slow, and was big enough to be two people, J.W. called him "The Slow Brothers."

But Jay wasn't amused. He wanted the lean and hungry type player, and Koonce wasn't that. He wanted aggressive, mean and nasty players, and Koonce wasn't that either.

Three days after we got smeared on Game of the Week, Chicago came to town and Jay decided to shake things up. He wanted Joe Kaiser, our starting pitcher, to "flip" Kyle LeMaster, the rookie Chicago outfielder who was hot at the time. So Kaiser chinned him the first time up and hit him in the ribs the second, and then the Chicago pitcher hit Kaiser when *he* came up and there was a fight.

When there's a baseball fight everybody runs out onto the field and you've got maybe forty guys standing around and four or five who really want to drive home a point. I was out there trying to avoid an argument and ran into Alex Ennis, who was hitting coach for Chicago by then. Alex was pulling Jay off somebody and I grabbed Alex from behind and he turned around and saw me.

"Little Tyke!" he boomed out. "Wanna duke it?"

I looked up at him. "Don't tangle with me, Alex," I warned him. "I'm trouble."

"We're too old for this," he said, swaying while some-body rolled into his ankles. "How you been?"

"All right," I said. "We oughta get together—"

"Fu-u-u-ck!" said Alex. Jay had swung loose from him, spun around and hit him in the belly. "Who's this hittin' me? Bates!" Alex grabbed Jay in a bear hug and lifted him off the ground. "Keep outta my gut, Bates. The Doc thinks I might have ulcerative colitis." He explained his symptoms while he held Jay off the ground and Jay's face turned purple.

The umps threw a few people out of the game, Jay prominently included. When he had his breath back he told me I was managing and to put Koonce in the game. "Tell him to stick it in LeMaster's ear. We gotta protect our players," he said. Then he went back into the runway to the locker room and I was in charge.

There's this ancient theory that pitchers are supposed to "protect" their teammates by retaliating if they're thrown at by the opposition. It's real simple, Old Testament baseball, eye-for-an-eye stuff. Not everybody be-lieves in it, but of course Jay did. His version was more like an eye and both ears and the tail for an eye.

Jay knew Koonce would get thrown out of the game if he hit LeMaster, but that was the idea; Jay didn't *care* if Koonce had to leave.

I didn't like my position. It was the first time I'd ever been asked to run a major league team, and my first order of business was to tell my pitcher to drill some-body. It was just the kind of situation I might have expected to find myself in, working for Jay. As a player I'd always been a good soldier, but this was different. I was more responsible.

Jay and I had always had a different outlook on the game. For one thing, I thought it *was* a game, and Jay didn't. If the objective was to skull the other guy, I thought, you might as well just take the bats and swing at each other and eliminate the ball altogether. I could understand pitching inside but I'd never cared for the idea of the high hummer to the head. Maybe I was just soft, like Jay suspected.

So I wasn't happy with my first chore as interim manager. I stood out on the mound next inning while Koonce was warming up and said to him, "Jay wants you to hit LeMaster when he comes up."

Koonce kept throwing and said, "Why? We started it an' now it's even."

I looked around and thought things over. When I get in a spot where I have to make some kind of choice involving morals or uncomfortable questions, I usually try to find a way to dodge through it without a head-on collision between right and wrong. It's kind of a weasely quality I have. When I see it in my son I sit him down for a half-hour speech.

So I considered it in my slippery way. On the one hand, Koonce probably couldn't hurt LeMaster too bad if he hit him—not with his stuff. On the other hand, if he knocked his earflap into his cortex I'd feel worse than a weasel.

"How about you jam him?" I finally said.

Koonce threw a breaking ball and said, "I can't throw hard enough to jam him."

Well, hell, I thought.

"Try to get it in on his fists, all right?" I told him, and walked back to the bench.

You know, the kid was right. He *couldn't* jam LeMaster. He tried his best fastball on the hands and LeMaster turned on it and yanked it so far I didn't see it start to go down; now that I'm older I lose sight of the really intercontinental blasts after they've gone about 450 feet. I'll need glasses in a year or two.

We lost the game and Jay called everybody together in the locker room afterward for what he called a "balls check."

He was standing in front of all of us, still in his uniform, practicing putts with a bat and laughing a little bit, like I'd seen him do once or twice before when he was really mad.

"Balls check," he said, swinging the bat like a pendulum. "Want you all to take a look down there and see if you've got any." He raised his head. "You looked, Koonce. Not too sure, were ya? Check real close, because I don't want any fucking handicapped players on my team. Could be you're a puss, is that true? They say first step in beating a problem is admitting you got it. So why don't you say what your problem is? If you're a puss, let's get it out so we can help you."

Koonce's face got red and he said, "You shouldn't talk to me that way."

"Whaddya gonna do about it, throw up?" said Jay.

Koonce started walking toward Jay, who put his bat down and got ready. I stepped in between them, hoping for company. Shain and Paris and John Turk came between, too, to break it up. Shain was saying, "C'mon, Slow, let's go over here," while I faced Jay. The six of us were all bumped up against each other like we were trying to dance in an elevator.

"My fault, Jay," I told him. "I just said to jam him."

Jay squinted at me while Paris and Shain walked Koonce backward. "That ain't what I told you to do," he said.

"I know," I admitted.

Jay's face registered a series of emotions, from disbelief to rage to his portrait of a man holding himself in. I could see he was struggling, trying to figure out what the down side of slugging his third-base coach might be. He finally decided to put his immediate impulse on hold.

Then he said, real softly—I may have been the only one who heard him—"You're a fuckin' joke," and went into his office.

That night, back in my apartment, I called Pat and we discussed the events of the day. When I got to the "balls check" part of my story, she said, "You should tell him that's my job." We speculated on how soon we'd be seeing each other; I thought it wouldn't be long.

Afterward I got to watching TV. There was a late-night movie on about guys on a construction site being attacked by a possessed bulldozer. The bulldozer would run around by itself, killing the construction workers. I like to watch movies about problems I'm never likely to have because they make me feel better, but this was totally unrealistic.

There was a knock on the door and when I opened it I saw Jay standing out in the hall.

He said, "Jessup says we should work this out."

"C'mon in."

Jay walked past me and stared at the television set. I offered him a beer and he took it, which was unusual, and watched the bulldozer run over one of the featured players in the film.

"You screwed up," he said.

I supposed I had, but I wasn't sure, so I didn't say anything.

"If you didn't like what I told you to do you shoulda said so," he said.

"That's true," I said.

The bulldozer had turned around and was chasing some guy through a field. "Your kind of movie," said Jay. "No driver."

I turned it off. "I been thinkin'," I said, "maybe I should move on."

Jay's face got bitter. "Jessup said you did the wrong thing but you had the right idea. He chewed my ass out about throwing at LeMaster again, said I was managing like a gangster. I'm on fucking probation. There's always somebody tellin' me what to do. I'll never have any clout until I win." He looked at me. "You've always thought you were better than me, haven't you?"

"Better at what?" I said.

"Just better. Guys who are better *off* think they're better *than*."

I didn't know what to say. I always *had* been better off than Jay. I'd always had more money and I had my own family, and I'd always been happier. I didn't go through life marveling at how happy I was but I knew I had to be happier than *Jay*. He'd always been going uphill and I'd always found myself on pretty level ground.

"I've looked into guys' faces all my life," he said, "who thought they were better than me. They got that look, like they're *civilized* and I'm lower down. Two things I hated about Tremayne back in Monmouth—one was the trick he played with that whore and the other was everything else about him. But mostly that fuckin' look, that 'I'm somebody, you ain't' look." He walked over to the kitchen counter and put his beer down.

"*You* had that look in the locker room, like you're Jesus Christ and I'm walking shit. You helped me in the old days, but—" he shook his head and said tonelessly, "it was hard, just standing there and not wiping that look off. Gave me a headache. I don't wanta see that look again."

"I don't always agree with you, Jay—" I began.

"I don't *give* a fuck!" he said suddenly. "I didn't say *agree*. You don't *agree*"—he twisted the word—"you tell me, and that's all about that."

"Maybe not," I said. "Maybe I don't want to work for somebody as *mean* as you are."

He looked at me for a second and made a little grimace; he didn't smile, but his eyes looked amused.

"You don't get it," he said. "You don't get why I want these guys to play crazy. One on one, crazy kills sane, hard kills soft. You want me to pat everybody on the ass."

"Some of these kids could *use* a pat on the ass."

Jay stood up straight and got brisk, walking to the door. "I ain't gonna talk about this anymore," he said. "We don't see things the same way. We both see a mountain, I want to climb it, you want to stop halfway up and live there. But you're coming the rest of the way."

"I don't know if I am," I said. Jay stopped at the door. He looked uncomfortable for the first time.

"Maybe you should quit. Maybe I'd like to *help* you quit. But Jessup reams me if you quit. He says I have to learn how to 'handle these differences.' " Jay shrugged, disgusted, and then said, in a resigned way, "I'll do this. You want Boys Town? Tomorrow I'll let Paris make out the lineup. We'll all play kiddie-ball, for one day. Tyke ball. Kisses and hugs. One day." His look at me was steady. "That's for the old days. But that's it. After that I'm in charge. I ain't gonna beg you to stay. And don't counter-fuckin'-dict me again."

"What about Koonce?" I asked.

Jay was firm. "Oh, no. He's gone. I got *that* much from Jessup. You got to pitch better than he does to be that much of a cluck."

Koonce got called in the next morning and was packed up and out and down to our farm team in Mesa by the time the rest of the players came in from taking infield. About a month later he was dealt to St. Louis in a minor league trade and I didn't see him again until September.

Paris made out the lineup card exactly as Jay would have except he put himself in the clean-up spot and moved Turk up to third so he might get better pitches. We got beat again. Jay shrugged, took over the next day and we started to win.

But Jay and I were in our final phase. You know how sometimes in a man-woman relationship somebody, usually the woman, will say, "I think we're drifting apart"? That wasn't the problem with Jay and me. The problem with Jay and me was that this year we'd drifted together.

12

WHEN THE RUSH STARTED WINNING AND MOV-
ing up through the standings in June and July, the press
started calling our way of playing "Bates-ball."

There really aren't that many different ways to play the
game. The rules prevent you from getting overly crea-
tive, just as in regular life the rules keep you from
moving up in the business world by murdering your su-
pervisor in front of witnesses. But there is sometimes
room in baseball for the innovative mind.

They've argued for years about how much difference a
manager makes, how many games he himself wins for his
team over the course of a year. Some people think of him
as a guy who can't win any, but can lose some if he's
stupid enough—like if he screws up the lineup or the
pitching staff. There are a few guys, however, who are
gifted enough to take marginal players and win with them,
and Jay was one of those.

His basic theory of play—bite, scream, kick, run-run-
run—was similar to that of other aggressive managers in
the past. But he added some things that had nothing to
do with percentages or playing by "the book." They had

to do with distraction, intimidation, breaking rhythm, unpredictability.

See, we were losing anyway. We were expected to lose. If we'd played like everybody else played, we would have *continued* to lose. But playing Jay's way, we just irritated the hell out of everybody, and we started to win. We also got back the crowds we'd been missing, and acquired a hard-core group of fans who called themselves "Rushians."

Jay believed in bad manners. Baseball has etiquette like any other profession, and when you ignore it, it grates on the other guy's nerves. He encouraged his players to do things that were the equivalent of singing while a golfer's on his backswing.

He had the guys steal when we were ahead by six runs. He had the pitchers work in an erratic rhythm; sometimes they'd get the ball back from the catcher and go right into their motion, other times they'd take a long pause. The hitters couldn't get their little batting rituals and practice swings timed right, and it annoyed them.

What annoyed them even more was when a dead-pull lefthanded hitter would be getting ready to rip one to right and our third baseman, Joe Surface, would sit down in the dirt before the pitch. Either the hitter would try to ignore him or he wouldn't; if he tried to change his swing to hit it past Surface, fine—he'd probably screw it up, and even if he hit it he wouldn't be hitting to his power.

Occasionally Jay would bring all the outfielders in and have them play right back of the infield with some musclehead kid at the plate. The kid would get all pumped

up and mad, take a mighty cut and dribble one ten feet
down the line or pop it up.

On offense, he had everybody running in weird situations, like when the catcher was tossing the ball back to
the pitcher. Once he signaled a triple steal against a
rookie catcher and the kid actually threw to a base instead of tagging the guy coming home—he was confused
by all the motion in his peripheral vision.

Jay didn't do this stuff all the time—there were certain
players he didn't try to distract, guys who were known to
be unflappable or who Jay considered dumb. "You can't
rattle a dummy," he would say. "He doesn't even notice
what you're doing." And as much as he loathed Davy
Tremayne, who still played a little, he would never
consider, say, bringing in the outfielders when Davy was
up because he knew Davy might just laugh and drill one
and Jay couldn't have stood it.

Jay gave our players some constructive, concrete help,
too. He studied all our hitters' blind spots when they batted
and fined them a buck every time they swung at a pitch in
that area. He gave back the bucks when they swung at a
hittable pitch, even if they missed it or popped it up.

But there's no question he was best at developing our
guerrilla attitude. "I don't want anybody looking forward
to playing us," he said. And pretty soon nobody did. We
were too fast and young and antagonistic. We didn't know
our place. We were bush. We might do any damn thing.
We didn't respect our betters, and often we played better
than our betters.

Winning feeds on itself. The more we improved, the
more we improved. In our early days of winning, the

players got excited and picked up their first true confidence in Jay as a manager. They liked the idea of sticking it to the established teams and getting famous. By mid-June he had them playing their little pumpers out.

As the media guys started to notice we were doing well, they got curious about Jay, and at some point in June the question of what "psychology" he used came up. I guess Jay did use psychology, but his knowledge of it was intuitive and basic—he sure didn't read up on it. One time we were in Jay's office after a win, Jay and me and a few players and a reporter. Everybody was feeling pretty good. The reporter was talking to Jay about how hard he had everybody playing and he asked, "Do you find yourself using psychology on the players to get them to perform?"

Jay did a little twitchy smile and said, "Sure. Ya got to. We do little tests to make sure everybody's got the right attitude."

"Like what?" asked the guy.

Jay looked around. "Oh . . ." he fixed his attention on an empty beer can on his desk and said, "Like that beer can."

"What about it?"

Jay looked at the reporter and said, "Do you think you could get it up your ass?"

There was a pause. The reporter looked a little flustered and said, "Why would I want to?"

"Well," said Jay, "that's where the psychology comes in."

Jay's players were expected to play "Bates-ball" even if they thought it was stupid at times. There was a play in a game in June that gave Jay a chance to make his philosophy real clear.

We were home against Houston, and Tony Biela was on first with one out when Paris hit one off the end of his bat, a soft little liner to the shortstop. Biela assumed it would be caught on the fly and decided to dive back into first, but the shortstop took it on one hop, stepped on second and threw to first to get Paris, who tripped over Biela as he crossed the bag. So we had two guys colliding at first on a double play—what the reporters call "zany" baseball.

For a second it looked like our big man, Paris, might be hurt, and Jay was beside himself. To me, Biela's decision had been reasonable—wrong, but reasonable. To Jay it was against nature.

"That's what happens when you're fucking *careful!*" he screamed down to Tony, who was rolling in pain on the ground behind the bag. "We don't run fucking *clockwise* on this team!"

"Paris spiked me," said Biela, gritting his teeth.

"He *shoulda* spiked you!" yelled Jay. "You're not supposed to *be* here, you dumb wop, we go *forward!* You don't go back before he catches the fucking ball!" Biela finally got up and limped back to the dugout, with Jay giving him an earful all the way.

If there was one play that crystallized for the team what Jay was all about, that one was it. He wanted forward motion. Run at them and maybe they'll flinch.

He had the right kind of players for his philosophy, too. Biela was older and inclined to play percentages, but the rest of the guys were young, and more like thugs. They liked Jay's style and adopted it.

We didn't have a very good bench, so Jay didn't use it much. He played the regulars almost every day, which meant they had a tendency to get worn out, especially since Jay was always after them to use all their available fuel in each game. We lost a couple tough ones in San Francisco in July and were about to lose a third when we got a big boost from John Turk.

John was the phlegmatic type, just played his game hard and didn't say much. In this one he led off the top of the ninth with us down by a run. The oh-one pitch was inside, he thought. So did I. The ump, Art Lemon again, said it was strike two. Our guys got on Lemon from the bench, but John didn't say anything. He hit the next pitch way over the wall in right, only his sixth home run of the year, to tie it up. Then he trotted around the bases and got thrown out of the game *as he crossed the plate* for directing a remark at Lemon.

Jay was just enormously impressed with John for that. He'd *never* been thrown out of a game that fast, much less after hitting one out. He was so flabbergasted he didn't even run out and argue with Lemon; he was all agog to find out what Turk had said to him. I think he thought John might have stumbled onto some rare, valuable cussword that Jay had overlooked in his travels or never heard. As it turned out all Turk had said was, "Where was *that* one, gutless?" which was practically Jay's theme song.

But seeing John hit it and then get the heave so rapidly gave the whole club a jolt, woke us up. We won in extra innings and kept winning on into August, playing better than we had any right to.

*   *   *

But an odd thing started happening. The more we won, the happier everybody got except Jay. Sunset Boone and Jessup, the fans and the local press, were all thrilled that we were winning when they'd all thought we'd lose, but it was slowly dawning on Jay that if this kept up, he might just have a chance to catch Davy Tremayne.

The truth, laid out in the standings, was that there wasn't really any reason we couldn't win the division. We were six games out on August 1, and St. Louis had lost their ace, Colorful Nickname Smith, for at least six weeks with a sore elbow. The closeness started eating at Jay.

He was like somebody who's been talking and talking about dating the homecoming queen and now finds that all her other possible escorts have been wiped out by food poisoning. Looks like he might wind up going out with her after all. To a certain mentality that brings up a worse set of problems than he had before.

Jay didn't confide in me as much as he used to by this time; I think he considered me soft, or even mushy. But one day before a game he told me, "I dreamed this morning that we caught him. And we were gonna play him in this big game and all the rules were different—we had to go on a quiz show to decide who won. I couldn't believe it. A quiz show! They asked me some question about geography, where some airport was or something, and I didn't know, so they took out a bat and hit a gong and out comes Tremayne from behind a curtain and says, 'Somewhere in Georgia,' and everybody claps and gives him the championship trophy. I said, 'Somewhere in

Georgia? What the fuck kind of answer is that?' And they
threw me off the show."

It can get to be a bad situation when a guy who always
took things too seriously kicks it up a notch. If Jay hadn't
told me about that dream I wouldn't have thought he got
any sleep at all.

The more we won in August, the more praise Jay got
from the press, the closer we got to St. Louis, the
grimmer and stranger he became. He began staring into
space in the middle of conversations and stopping in the
middle of sentences. He'd look bug-eyed at nothing for
long periods. It was worse when we won a game than
when we lost; if we won he was that much closer to
Tremayne and still not close enough.

If we'd gone into a major, grade-A slump and dropped
ten or twelve in a row to fall out of it, he might've been
better off. But we never did. We never lost more than
two in a row for a whole month, and Jay kept tightening
up. He even lost weight, and he didn't have any to spare.
He just had no mental or physical cushions on him. There
was nothing but edges.

In mid-August I took a look at the schedule and saw
again that our last three games were at home, against St.
Louis. That hadn't seemed particularly important early in
the year, but it was starting to take on significance. I
mentioned it to Jay a day later and he looked at me like I
should be delivering papers on my velocipede.

"You take a lot of time to figure things out, don't ya?"
he said.

*   *   *

Funny thing: Right about then I *was* taking time to figure some things out. I remember I spent one afternoon counting up how much time I had left until I was eighty. My fortieth birthday was coming up. I was hitting the back nine, and it made me think about just how temporary an immortal I was.

I wouldn't call it a crisis, exactly. I didn't want to switch careers, or women, or chuck everything and do what I'd always wanted, because I'd pretty much always *done* what I'd always wanted. I just began to worry about how much longer I could do it. It seemed to me that by the time I was eighty I'd've been asked to remove myself from baseball on the major league level, and I imagined Pat would be tired of me by that point, if not sooner. So I looked at eighty as the end and started computing how much of this and that I had between now and then.

For instance, everybody knows, I hope, that from forty years old to eighty is forty years, but not everybody knows it's 14,600 days. When I figured that out I got a little alarmed, because put that way it didn't seem like very much. Fourteen thousand days *isn't* very much, when you consider it's basically the rest of your life—if you're lucky—and you think about how many days will come afterward when you're no longer in the picture, the days you'll miss, which is all of them.

I realized I'd have to pay closer attention to those days as they went by and appreciate them more, otherwise I'd look up a few thousand days later and there I'd be—done, to my surprise.

I also decided to count up the hours and minutes I had between forty and eighty, hoping that a larger number would comfort me and make me feel like I had more time. The number of hours came out to 350,400, which still, somehow, didn't seem like much. I'd assumed I had a million hours left, at least, but I don't have anywhere near.

Now the amount of *minutes* between forty and eighty *is* a hefty number, something like 21 million, and that was the total I chose to concentrate on. It settled me down a bit to know that I had a few million *somethings* left before I turned eighty.

But all this calculation brought one thing forcibly home to me, and that was that whoever first said life is short was an expert analyst. I wasn't exactly on Death Row, but there was a limited amount of everything left, including ballgames, and the number, in most cases, was smaller than I'd thought it was when I didn't *know* what it was. And realizing those limits made me speculate some on just how much I wanted to spend my remaining days and hours and minutes in the company of Jay Bates.

It wasn't that Jay was making my life miserable; he was just being his usual self, only more so. And I didn't want to leave him before the end of the season, anyway; the race was getting too interesting and I liked our kids. But it occurred to me that prolonged personal contact with old Jay might reduce my longevity, or at least my enjoyment of it. I guess I'm like a lot of people who turn forty and look around at their nearest neighbor in the office or at home and say, "With the time I have left, do I want to be seated next to you?"

*   *   *

I was seated next to Jay in the clubhouse one afternoon
near the end of August and we saw an interview with
Davy Tremayne on a sports channel baseball show. The
interviewer asked Davy if he thought St. Louis had to
worry about the Rush. Davy was accustomed to talking to
these guys; he was as smooth as my son's chin.

" 'Course we do, Ray," he said, "but we should be all
right. We've got several players who've been in a pennant race before and that helps come September."

"What do you think of the job Jay Bates has done over
there?"

Davy smiled. "Well, y'know, Jay and I go way back."
He looked at the camera. "How ya doin', Jay? We played
together in the minors. Jay knows his baseball and I
admire what he's done with the Rush. But they're still a
few games back, so I'd rather be us than them, and I'd
rather be me than him." He grinned out at the viewers.

I looked over at Jay. His face was sort of blotchy and
he was staring back at the TV. I imagined he was counting the days, too.

13

IN A REAL WAR, I SUPPOSE THE SOLDIERS MIGHT hesitate to go into battle behind an officer with a little propeller on top of his helmet. And our guys weren't slow to notice when Jay began acting peculiar coming up on September.

Since he wasn't sleeping much he was so tired out that he'd go into little trances in his office and even on the bench during games. He wouldn't hear you then unless you poked him in the shoulder and repeated what you said. Then like as not he'd say something that didn't have to do with the matter at hand.

One time he spent most of a game on the bench talking about his childhood. He said the kids in his gang in Gary used to stop any kid with glasses on the street and take the glasses off his face and sell them back to him, daily. "My old man told me I was a shitheel who'd never amount to anything unless I changed," Jay said. "But I never changed. I'm still a shitheel." Then he giggled.

I could see the players give each other little sidelong looks—you know, the kind that say, "This guy is getting a little overripe."

But it's like they say—screwballs are crazy if they lose and eccentric if they win. People forgive a lot of kinks in a winner, and right about this time Jay suddenly got on a streak where every move he made was successful, whether it made sense or not.

He triple-shocked me in one game, when Paris was batting with guys on first and second and nobody out. It's a bunt situation for most hitters, but you don't ask your power hitter to bunt. On this occasion Jay did three things that went from improbable to screwy to ridiculous:

1. He had me give Paris the bunt sign.

2. When Paris bunted foul, Jay got so mad, apparently, that he yanked Paris out of the game and put in a pitcher to pinch-bunt.

3. He took off the bunt sign and let the pitcher swing away.

This is like managing from the Home for the Perpetually Mistaken. I was so busy staring at Jay in disbelief that I almost missed it when the pitcher doubled in two runs.

He'd sit on the bench when San Francisco was in the field against us and call every pitch before it came. He somehow had their signs figured out no matter what they did. He'd flash the pitch to me and I'd give it to our hitters; we always knew what was coming. Jay would laugh about it on the bench, which antagonized the San Francisco manager. After one of these games Paris and I were in Jay's office and I asked Jay how he knew all the signs even when they were changed. He said, "I got my fingers on the guy's brain. I read it like the blind people do."

When Paris and I left Darrell muttered, "It's like the Bat-Cave in there, ain't it?"

It was not rational, but he was *right* all the time. He must have somehow tapped into the game rhythm. There've been times in the past when I've felt during a game that I could tell what was going to happen, and I was right, but those times were rare. Jay was doing it regularly. The more tired and wasted he got, the more he could just *tell* what to do, even if he didn't seem to be paying attention. And whatever he did would work, and we'd win, and after the game he'd be miserable.

We drew the crowds, bigger all the time. Everybody wanted to come out and see Bates-ball. Jay got an ovation every time he walked out onto the field. Sunset Boone was thrilled; he was making money; Jessup was being called a genius for drafting all the live kids; and Jay above all was the miracle man. In the papers they compared him to Napoleon and Rommel and Robert E. Lee and all kinds of great tacticians. I got to thinking maybe he really was a genius—geniuses are supposed to be strange and have that glassy look.

Our little one-on-one relationship had pretty much eroded by this time. Jay didn't really talk to me anymore. I think he considered himself to be on a different mental plane from me, which was true enough. Sometimes I'd be talking to a player about something and I'd catch Jay looking at me with a funny sort of smirk on his face. After one of these times he walked up to McDevitt and said, "Ever notice how ninety-nine percent of what everybody says is horseshit?"

Our final dustup occurred after a win in Houston on August 29, the night we pulled to within four games and

Jay finally realized the players considered him an unpopped kernel. When the game was over Jay went into one of his walking trances, wandering through the clubhouse half-undressed, muttering and not seeing anything. He meandered around awhile and then came out of it to see Tom Gonder, the catcher, walking behind him and imitating him. At first he didn't get what Gonder was doing, staggering around with his eyes bugged out. Gonder practically bumped into him before he noticed that Jay was awake now.

Jay said, "What the hell's the matter with you, Gonder?"

Tom backed up a bit, embarrassed for a second, then grinned and said, "Nothin', skip. I'm just pretending I'm managing."

It was harmless enough, really; any manager knows, or should know, that the players needle him and talk behind his back and imitate him sometimes. It's irresistible. What upset Jay so much was that Gonder looked disturbed when he did it, which Jay took to be a reflection on his own mind. Which it was. So he took one step for the money and two for the show and punched Gonder in the mouth. I went to grab him, along with some other people, and he socked me too.

Well, you know, I'd seen that punch coming for twenty years and I *still* couldn't get out of the way. I suppose I was lucky, because he wasn't planted too well and hadn't been at full strength lately, but he had all the old rage behind his swing. He got me pretty square and split my upper lip. Later it swelled up like a rubber raft. I went down on my ass and Jay yelled at me while he was being held by two players and another coach.

"You guys think I'm crazy?" he shrieked. "You think I'm crazy, Tyke?"

I got up slow. I couldn't talk right. I felt like my lip had been mooshed back in between my teeth. "I don't think you got very good control of yourthelf," I said.

"Lemme go," said Jay to the guys holding him, but they didn't. "I ain't gonna do nothin', lemme *go*, goddamnit!" He struggled loose and stood there, panting at me.

"Get the hell outta here, Tyke, you're done," he said.

"Ahh, fuck you, Jay," I said. He went to hit me again but Paris caught his arm, thank goodness. I was worried about my front teeth.

When we got back to Santa Rita, Jay and I were called into Jessup's office for a last talk, the gist of which was that it was bad form for a coach to get bounced off a team during the season and why couldn't we work things out.

Sunset Boone was there, looking genuinely puzzled and pained, like we were a couple of hombres who'd tried to take the law into our own hands. "Thought you boys were saddle pals," he said. "What happened?" He looked at me and I started to say this good phrase I'd often seen in the paper to describe one guy hating another guy, but it was coming out "philothophical differentheth," so I stopped halfway through.

Jay said, "Charlie thinks there's an easy way to do hard things." I missed his next two or three statements wondering whether that first one was true, then woke up as I heard Jay say, "He was undermining me with the players."

"I didn't undermine you," I said.

"You told them not to pay any attention to me, and in my book that's undermining."

"I told them not to pay attention when you called them *ath*-holeth!" I said indignantly.

"When I give a sign and you stare at me from the box like I just told you to piss on the baseline it looks horse-shit," said Jay. "The players see stuff like that. It's bad for morale."

I don't think there've been too many managers who cared less about "morale" than Jay, but I didn't see much point in arguing. I *had* stared at him a few times when he'd flashed what I thought was an especially odd sign, wondering if I'd gotten it right. And it was clear from the way Sunset and Jessup were acting that Jay was going to get his way on this one. Jessup had demanded before the season that Jay stay on an "even keel," but when you're winning you can list quite a bit to starboard before any-body cares. Even Tom Gonder wasn't sore at Jay for slugging him, and had apologized for his imitation.

"I never meant to undermine Jay," I said, "but if he thinkth I did . . ." I shrugged. "I oughta move on."

Jessup shrugged too, with his eyebrows. "Perhaps it's for the best. I'm not condoning brawling, Jay. I don't want any more of it. But if your differences can't be resolved, and Charlie feels he should explore other ave-nues, so be it."

And so it was. We agreed not to use the words "fired" or "quit" to the press; Jessup suggested "philosophical differences." I got up and shook hands with him and Sunset. I told Sunset I was sorry we were no longer pardners.

"Vaya con Dios," he said.

"Yeah, well . . ." I looked down at Jay, who remained seated.

"What the hell, Jay," I said. "Good luck, I gueth."

His eyes flicked up at me and away. "Sure," he said. He shifted in his seat with the desire to get on to new topics. I was gone.

I flew back to Chicago the next day, one of the few times when I was on a plane without a bunch of ballplayers giving the stewardesses a hard time. J. W. Shain used to rev up a special look for the stews when they came by, what he called his Care-Bear Stare. It started as a fixed gaze meant to represent smoldering sensuality and picked up passion until he was quivering uncontrollably in his seat. J.W.'s belief in its hypnotic power never wavered, even when the women would speed up to get by him.

At first on that flight I was just relieved to have come to the end with Jay. No more phone calls, no more dreams, no more watching the fuse burn down to the cherry bomb. Working with Jay I'd found myself getting tired of baseball, and that was no good for me.

I don't know how many principles I have. Not a big list. But I do have an outlook. My outlook on baseball was that it was beautiful and balanced, and in my mind and memory I was a collector of ballgames. The games were like diamonds or fingerprints, all of a piece but no two alike, and you put them all together in a string and you had a season, the seasons in a string and you had a life. They were battles, sure, but not to the death. Even the losses went in my game collection and after a while they could be remembered without much pain. Baseball was a struggle, but not war—a game. *Pretend* war. To Jay, of course, there was nothing pretend about it.

To somebody like Davy Tremayne, who'd always been successful at it, the game was an art form, where the pieces always fell into place and you had the leisure to think about little curlicues like whether people played according to their names. It had always been more of a scuffle for me than for Davy, but if I had to place myself in attitude I'd put myself closer to him than Jay.

It looked now, though, as if my baseball life might finally be behind me. Since I'd first been traded as a player I'd never kept a job with anybody longer than a season, and now I'd come up short even of that. I looked out the window of the plane and saw my next step as being right through the cloud cover and down to earth in a hurry.

It gave me a good, solid, clammy rush of panic—the kind where every thought leaves your mind except the one that comes over the loudspeaker and says, "You're in the shit now, Charlie." It's strong; you get a physical reaction, your face gets hot and cold alternately. I'd had it before.

When I was still a minor leaguer I worked one Christmas season for the post office in Quincy. They'll hire a gorilla at Christmas time. For most of the two weeks I was there I was sorting mail and helping load trucks and stuff, but one day they gave me a route and I was a mailman. Just for the one day.

I had my mailbag and I was walking around a residential area I didn't know too well, slipping and falling in the snow and ice while the mail in my hand went up in the air and came down in the snow so the ink on the envelopes got nice and runny and hard to read.

I had a mailbox key, and on my route I was supposed to stop at the mailboxes on some of the corners and open them up and take the mail out of them. So I'm slipping and sliding and staggering along with my mailbag, which was heavy, and delivering my Christmas cards and magazines, and I get to one of my corner mailboxes and go to open it and find that I no longer have my key.

I got that same rush of panic then. I'd been told to be sure and not lose that key, because if one got lost they had to spend a trillion dollars to change the locks on all the boxes all over town, it was a federal law or something. And somewhere in the five blocks since I'd left the last box, somewhere in the snow, I knew that key was sitting, till spring.

It was cold that day, but while I retraced my steps I was sweating like the nineteen-year-old fuckup that I was, looking for a hole in the snow about the size of the edge of a quarter. I found the spots where I'd fallen and made a little design on the ground, but no key. I thought about what they'd say at the post office when I went back and told them. I thought about running away but I didn't know what to do with the mail. I'd be arrested if I didn't deliver the mail.

I didn't know if I'd passed the spot where I'd dropped the key or not; I just stared at the snow all the way back to the last mailbox, and there was the key in the lock, where I'd left it. I felt like I'd been saved to do something great in life. I think I set a record that day for covering my route slower than anyone ever had before, but I didn't care, I had my key.

My panic now, on the plane, reminded me of my panic then, and as I recovered enough to consider what I might do with the rest of my life, I thought about becoming a mailman. At least I had experience.

Pat and Jamie met me that night at O'Hare and I told Pat she could kiss me anywhere but on the mouth. Jamie thought I looked real funny and I imagine I did. I'd never been so glad to get home in my life.

"I think you married a guy who missed his chance in the grocery business," I said to Pat.

"Why don't you try baseball?" she said.

"Who'll try *me?*"

"Dave Tremayne wants you in St. Louis. He called while you were in the air and said he needs an expert on the Jay Bates way of thinking."

Well, it wouldn't take more than a minute to tell Davy I'd figured out Jay was the unpredictable type. But it *was* a way to put off going through the classifieds. I sniffed the air experimentally and got a whiff of Davy Tremayne and St. Louis. The thweet thmell of thucktheth.

EVERY NEW BALLCLUB IS A NEW FOSTER FAM-
ily, and you never know how long you're going to last
with any of them. You can kind of grow up in one home,
getting close to everyone, and then find out you've been
adopted by somebody else and you've got a whole new
set of temporary brothers.

I went to St. Louis on September second, pessimistic
about how long I'd be retained if all Davy wanted was a
Jay Bates expert. I figured that if the Rush dropped out
of the race all of a sudden I'd be "discharged," as Casey
Stengel used to say, and back at the orphanage before
the first day of fall.

Davy Tremayne took me directly from the airport to
his own restaurant, "Tremayne's," not far from the
river. Needless to say, we had a good table. Davy's
waiters had the dual duties of serving the customers and
telling them not to ask him for autographs when he was
eating.

My steak dinner was on him, and to add to the appeal
of that arrangement it was fresh and delicious. I appreciated that because when I'm home I have to economize

and make use of all the leftover meat; the slogan at my house is "It May Be Gray But It Smells Okay."

When we first sat down, Davy said, "Sounds like you and Jay were developing a battering relationship on the Rush, with Jay as the batter." He looked at me with some anxiety and said, "Get it?"

When I said I did, he seemed relieved. "Good," he said. "Half the guys on my club never know what the hell I'm talking about. At least when I'm with you I can be myselves."

He was getting a little gray in his hair, and he said he had a headache, which surprised me; I didn't know he was capable of one. For a change, Davy looked like he had his share of worries.

For one thing, his recent marriage to Shana McKenzie, the news anchor he'd met when he played in New York, had already busted up. Shana had become the first woman in that state, I believe, to have a divorce awarded to her on the grounds of Peter Pan Syndrome. On top of that, Davy wasn't turning out to be infallible as a manager.

Often when a superstar starts running a club he gets subjected to criticism he was immune to as a player. The press and fans in St. Louis were getting on Davy a bit because they thought he should've had the division race locked up by now; they were irritated that the Rush wouldn't fold up and go away. It had to be *somebody's* fault, and St. Louis was Davy's team.

"A couple years ago," he said, "my agent tried to get Hollywood interested in a TV movie about me. We figured it could come out next year when I get my three-thousandth hit. It was gonna be based on my book—did you read my book?"

"Oh, yeah," I said. Actually I'd sort of skimmed it. It was one of those "as told tos," and it was okay, I guess. I was only in it on page fifty-seven, referred to as a lifelong friend Davy had made in the minors. Then I vanished. "Lifelong" and "booklong" are not the same.

"So we're trying to move my story," Davy continued, "and all the producers turned it down. They said there was no drama in it because I never had any setbacks. Pretty soon they may be more interested."

He talked about marriage briefly, expressing astonishment that so many people actually sustained one. "Lemme ask you something," he said. "Do you ever find yourself getting *tired?*"

"Of Pat? How could I? I've only seen her four times in the last seven months."

"What about in the winter?"

"Well . . ." I thought about it. "I *like* Pat."

Davy shook his head and pushed his salad around. "Shana felt that just the one personality is all you have to have, forever. She was always the same. She told me I either had too *many* personalities or not enough." He leaned back in his chair. "Maybe marriage should be like free agency. You sign up for anywhere from one to three years and then you've got the option to renew or move on, y'know? Why insist on this self-renewing contract? Isn't it just what we're fighting against in every other walk of life?"

"Did the divorce put a dent in your chances for twenty-five million?" I asked.

"Oh, well," he said.

Davy guided me through a list of the injuries his pitching staff had suffered in the last month. Aside from Lefty Smith, he'd lost his number-two starter, Frank Hooker, with a pulled hamstring, and his bullpen closer, Tom Feathers, with one of those freak injuries that come whenever you think nothing else can happen. Davy still seemed to be in shock about it.

"Feathers loves movies, all right?" he said. "Especially the ones with the old-time comedians. He's got tapes of all the old Laurel and Hardys. So last weekend he's out in the driveway showing his son how Oliver Hardy would close the trunk of his car, and he jams his finger and now he can't throw. It took me twenty minutes to get him to admit how he did it." Davy splayed his fingers out and down and emphatically bumped them once on the tabletop. "Another fine mess. Now I got no closer. I could understand his pretending to be somebody else, but why pretend to be a fuckup?"

I told him about Tom Gonder pretending to be Jay Bates and Jay's reaction to it.

"Sounds like Jay's finally feeling the strain," said Davy. "Doesn't keep him from winning, though. Even with our injuries I never figured he'd be this close. I just naturally assumed he'd bust one of those little veins in his temple by now—I never thought I'd be running down the stretch with his teeth in my butt. What the hell is he doing over there, anyway? He doesn't play percentages or use the book. He's managing like *Norman* Bates."

"He doesn't like patterns," I said. "He wants everything random, like. The only thing you can count on him to do is push—he's got everybody running."

149

"How did he give you signs? I couldn't pick it up."

"Sometimes with his legs, just pumping them up and down a certain way. Sometimes he didn't give them at all—he had other guys on the bench do it. But he'll change all that now anyway, with me here." I hesitated, then decided to get it over with. "I don't know how much help I can be. If you're looking for somebody to tell you the next thing Jay's gonna do, you need a gypsy. I'd be guessing just like everybody else."

"I'll get some use out of you," Davy said confidently.

We talked a bit about the pitchers Davy had down in Triple A. I only knew a couple of them.

"Most of them are worse than what I've got," he said, "but we might as well bring 'em up since it's September. What about this Fabian Koonce? You had him for a while."

"Good control, not much stuff," I said. "No heat."

"Think he could get Jay's kids out?"

"No. Not from what I saw. But he wouldn't walk anybody either."

Davy sighed. "He sounds like half of a good pitcher. Great name, though."

Names were still important to Davy, I found after I'd been with the club a few days. He seemed to have more confidence in guys whose names struck him as suitable. He wouldn't play a bad player with a good name over a good player with a bad one, but he had a habit of *adjusting* the names of some guys to fit his image of the successful athlete. He called his catcher, Ralph Hartman, "Hurricane" Hartman to make him sound more dynamic than he in fact was. "Hurricane" did have a fine arm, but the rest of him was sluggish.

There were some names on the squad that Davy couldn't do anything with, though. His number-three starter was a big guy, Howard Seeburger—the kind of name Davy associated with a losing record. And Howard *hadn't* been pitching well lately. Davy had tried calling him "King Kong" Seeburger to make him feel more forceful out there on the mound, but so far Howard hadn't responded in any positive way.

Aside from his little name game, which seemed harmless to me, Davy was a solid representative of the "book" manager, who makes his moves according to reason and logic and sits back and watches them work however many percent of the time they're supposed to.

Talking to Davy that first night in St. Louis was a relief. It was restful to sit and chat with a manager who didn't seem to be fighting the urge to leap across the table at me. This, I thought, was more like it. In all the years since Monmouth it was the first time I'd ever been on the same side as Davy Tremayne. It felt good; it felt *normal,* which was important to me at that time. I like regular room temperature, not a lot of seething and boiling in the air.

The last thing Davy asked me that night was whether I felt uncomfortable about switching allegiances so fast, from Jay to him.

"Well," I said after a moment, "it's baseball. New home, new family. We all move around. Besides, I think Jay was telling me when he socked me that he wanted me somewhere else."

"I never hit my people," Davy assured me. "It's unimaginative."

*   *   *

Davy decided he wanted me in uniform, as a substitute for Bud Metzger, his third-base coach, who had to have gall bladder surgery.

I could sympathize with old Bud. I had surgery myself once, for a hernia, when I was a player, and will state that coming out from under the anesthetic was truly a rude awakening. I remember my blood pressure went down and I felt all floppy; people started running around snapping out orders on how to stabilize me. I felt a whole lot more like I had a hernia after it was repaired than I had when I had it. They gave me some Demerol and Pat read to me out of *The Baseball Encyclopedia*—conclusive proof that she loved me. She's always found that book the most boring assemblage of numbers ever compiled, but her concern for me overcame her revulsion for its contents and she kind of crooned to me while I lay there in the bed about how Earl Webb hit sixty-seven doubles in 1931, and so on. Eventually the stats piled up in the air around us and put us both to sleep. That woman has sacrificed her intellect for me more than once, but that particular instance is one I'll always treasure.

Having had surgery myself I didn't want to push Bud onto the table unless he definitely had to go, but as it happened he did, and Davy offered me a choice: I could either coach third or I could coach first and he'd move his first-base coach over to third.

Well, it was an easy decision. Coaching first just isn't nearly as fun and challenging as coaching third. In fact it's not even really as challenging as walking the dog. You can kind of disappear in that job. On a veteran team like St. Louis, the first-base coach is present mostly for the sake of symmetry. When the hitters get on base they may give you their batting gloves, but they don't need much in the way of advice on how to live their lives between first and second. About the biggest responsibility you have over there is making sure that whenever it's a close play and your man gets called out and argues, *you're* the one who gets thrown out of the game, not him.

So I chose the third-base assignment and took a crash course from Bud in the new signs so I wouldn't be giving the Rush hit-and-run to a St. Louis player who was supposed to bunt. It wasn't difficult; with Davy's hitters the main sign was "whack it."

A couple days after I joined my new family I got a phone call in my hotel room one night, and when I answered a voice said, "Izzis Tremayne's boyfriend?"

Jay sounded odd on the phone. Well, not odd; he sounded shitfaced. That didn't make any sense to me until he told me he was on medication for his insomnia—Jessup had made him see a doctor. He certainly talked as though he was under the influence of some kind of mixture. I don't believe he'd have called me at all if he hadn't exceeded the recommended dosage.

It was late where he was, which made it two hours later where I was, and I'd been asleep, so neither of us was at his best. I lay there in bed with my head on the receiver and the receiver on my pillow for a bit while Jay told me the Rush had won that night and he'd known all along I'd wind up working for Davy. Then he said, "You been spillin' your guts to Tremayne about my signs? I changed 'em. I got Leo Keeler coachin' third now. We ain't missin' a beat."

"Well, I'm glad to hear it," I said.

"Fuckin' A," he said. He liked the sound of that and said it again. Then there was a pause, and then he said, "So now you're a store dummy for his millionaires. How you feel about walkin' out on our guys? You shoulda stayed over here."

"I thought you wanted me out, Jay."

"Ahhh, maybe I shoulda kept ya," he said, "but ya gotta see my side. After I popped you I coulda asked ya to stay, but all I *really* wanted to do was kick your ass some more. See what I mean?"

"Sure," I said.

"I just can't stomach guys like you, guys who say things like 'Take it easy,' " he said, and then began a whiny imitation of the way he felt guys like me sounded. " 'Why'n'tcha take it *easy?* Why'n'tcha look at the birds in the sky an' the leaves on the trees an' the flowers in the, in the garden?' "

"I don't remember ever saying—"

"Well, I don't think about the birds in the sky," Jay went on. "I just think about the standings." He stopped talking for a few moments. Then he said, "You can have first shot at me next time."

I thought that was a nice gesture on Jay's part and I told him so. He said, "Then I'll beat the shit outta ya. You're lucky I just hit ya the once, y'know. You had it comin' more'n that. Now you and Tremayne can sit around and take it easy together. I'm gonna come and get ya, though. I got all the momentum. You ain't got any pitching, ya noticed that yet?"

"Maybe not, but we got three games on *you,*" I said.

"Well, you got first shot at me next time," he said. He sounded like he was just hitting his stride and might say it four or five more times.

"You oughta get some sleep, Jay," I said.

"I don't know what it is with these pills," he muttered. "They're s'posed to knock me out but they only make me stupid."

"Give 'em a chance," I said.

"All right, the hell with ya then."

"Hey, Jay, wait a minute," I said, thinking he was about to sign off. There was something I wanted to tell him that I'd never gotten around to saying before our bustup. "I just want you to know," I said, "that I think you've done one helluva job with the Rush."

"No shit," he said, and hung up.

Now that I was with my new relatives I decided I'd appreciate my new advantages. When you change positions you work it out in your mind so you're better off, and I figured life would be more pleasant with St. Louis. Maybe not as exciting, but not as feverish, either. Fewer thrills but fewer spills, was my forecast.

I remember when Jamie was about seven, one day he asked me if he was going to grow hair on his face when he got older. I assumed he was looking forward to it, and I told him, absolutely, he'd grow hair on his face just like Daddy. And then he said he didn't want to.

It seems that he'd decided on that day that he didn't want to get older at all. He was satisfied with the way things were. Up to then he'd always been a kid with plans, to be a fighter pilot or a toy manufacturer when he grew up, but on this day he'd reached a little patch in his life where he no longer liked the idea of progress.

I'd had several changes in the last few years. I was hoping for some stability in Never-Land with Davy Tremayne. For the time being I didn't want to grow any more hair on my face either.

15

DAVY'S CLUB WAS ALL MUSCLE AND SHINE IF you didn't count the pitchers. While the players on the Rush had gradually developed a kind of exhausted drive, like some car salesmen have, the St. Louis regulars seemed to swagger wherever they went.

Besides Davy at second, Hurricane Hartman at catcher and George Washington in center, there was a typical set-up of Ted Grim at third, Garry Perry at short and Ray Kazanski at first, with John Casale and Hector Herrera in left and right. All those last five could hit twenty homers a year, and Casale and Kazanski could do you thirty and up.

Kazanski had the attitude they all had—businesslike, confident, maybe a little arrogant. When he greeted me on my first day in the clubhouse he shook hands and said, "I hope you're not one of these coaches who feels like he has to tell people what to do."

The regulars just didn't think they needed supervision. They saw no reason why winning shouldn't be a routine part of their day as long as they were left alone and the pitchers didn't give up ten runs a game. There was no racial clique on the team that I could see—it was more like a quality-control clique. The regulars were the elite troops and everybody else was welcome to stay out of their way and tag along for the postseason money.

These guys were all slick fielders, even the big ones like Casale and Kazanski. Maybe they'd studied Davy, who, old as he was, could still pick it at second. He had the most graceful tag on steal attempts in the league; it was a sweeping, fluid swipe at the ground in front of the bag that always kicked up dust and looked so authoritative that the umps gave him calls even when the runner beat him.

The only flaw I could spot in the defense was that George Washington, although fast, had a habit of skidding out and losing his footing a lot in the outfield; the other players called him "Slip." That little drawback aside, St. Louis had the best starting eight anywhere, batting and fielding.

But our pitchers ruined the overall effect. With the pitchers we had left, we were like a magazine cover girl with brown teeth. Whenever we were in the field and I was in the dugout watching, I wanted to grab a bat and get up there myself. I was sure I could hit King Kong Seeburger and all the rest of our guys except Todd Briggs, and it wasn't necessary to hit *him*.

Briggs was one of those young, talented wild men who throw so many pitches out of the strike zone that his fielders can feel their lives ebbing away out there while they wait for him to get one over. Davy lost patience with him when Briggs was working the second inning of a game in my first week. The kid walked two guys and then somehow got all tangled up with himself on his delivery and threw the ball straight down into the ground. Besides being extremely embarrassing, that's a balk. The runners moved up and the hitter singled them in and Davy sent Briggs off the mound.

That night Davy told me, "I'm gonna start that Koonce kid once. I'd rather see the ball in play all the time than watch Briggs stepping on his dick out there. I gotta get a rest from it. He pitches like he's got a shower head on the end of his arm."

Fabian had been called up right after the first of the month, along with some other kids. I was happy to greet him when I first saw him in the clubhouse, back up in the bigs for at least a little while. His face was so open and blank it reminded me of when Jamie was a week old.

"I want to thank you," he told me, "for taking my part when Jay Bates treated me like corn smut."

"Well, we both got kicked outta that state, didn't we?" I said. "Least now we're closer to home."

"Hey, you know the skip here?"

"Yeah, we go back a ways."

"Well, maybe you can tell me," said Koonce. "I can't tell if he's havin' me on or what. I can't understand him. He told me I got a great future 'cause I got the best name on the staff. What's *that* mean?"

"Means he likes ya. You're not corn smut to him."

We all kept track of the Rush, and they kept pace with us. Seemed like all the close ones were going Jay's way. He'd win on an overthrow or a bad hop or a bases-loaded walk—the kind of wins you get by keeping the pressure on. Jay was still playing his regulars every day, and they should have been huffing and puffing by this time of year, but there was no sign of it yet. It made me wonder whether they and Jay had enough adrenaline to take them all the way before they finally collapsed. I wondered how long they could really go at 110 percent.

As September went along we played the Rush pretty even, but we couldn't add to our lead. We'd annihilate somebody 19–6 one day and get beat 11–8 the next, while Jay's guys played all the 2–1 and 3–2 games. Everybody in the division had dropped away but the Rush; it was just us two. The other races weren't real close, so Jay and Davy became the big baseball news.

When a couple of teams are going to the wire together the papers like to match them up, compare them to each other in their stories, like they do with prizefighters. They set it up as if two strong men are meeting each other on Main Street and here's the size of each guy's biceps and how long his inseam is. The media were doing a lot of such comparisons in September between our pitchers and their pitchers and our hitters and their hitters, and they took special interest in the match-up between our manager and their manager.

It had come to the notice of the nation's press that Jay Bates was an unusual character, so now everybody was starting to diagnose him in the papers. A writer for a big national syndicate called Neatly Chiseled Features did a profile on him; you might have seen it. It was titled: "Jay Bates of the Rush—He'll Beat Ya or Delete Ya."

I thought that was the wrong kind of encouragement to give somebody like Jay, but I wasn't consulted on the title. Often, it seems, the writers look for the blood-thirsty angle when they're covering baseball; they prefer it when "there is no love lost between these two teams" and so on. Jay was right up their street.

When they found out he was taking medication it built into a big story. Somebody asked Sunset Boone how he felt about his manager "taking downers," and Sunset said, "The way he's going I'd just as soon send a bottle of his pills to all my players." Everybody got all upset about the quotation and Sunset had to call a press conference to say he'd only been pretending he was Abraham Lincoln and that he wouldn't have made the remark if he'd known everybody was going to act like horses in a burning barn about it.

I got extra attention from the reporters because I'd worked for each side during the year. I had never been such an object of interest to them before. They wanted my opinion on *every*thing—but mostly on Jay and his mental makeup.

I didn't care for the questions. I wasn't qualified to answer them, for one thing, and for another I didn't want to accidentally make a comment that would crank Jay and the Rush up even more than they already were. I usually didn't say anything at all about him, but I forgot this prudent policy when I got collared by my brother-in-law on our last trip to Wrigley with two weeks left in the season. It was a Friday and we had a three-game lead at the time.

You'd think somebody in your own family would be considerate enough to let you do your yoga or whatever you do before a big game, but Ron Dempsey's a diligent reporter; he'd ask you for a statement while you were having a seizure.

Behind the batting cage that day he asked me, "Is it true that you called Jay Bates crazy and that's why he slugged you?"

"No," I said, "I *never* called Jay crazy."

"Not even kidding? Like saying, 'You're crazy,' in an offhand way?"

"Nope," I said, "I'm sure I never did. In fact," I added stupidly, "I would've made it a point not to."

Maybe you've heard of lawyers in court "pouncing" on a witness's statement. Well, Ron pounced on mine.

"Why?" he asked eagerly. "Is he sensitive about things like that?"

"No," I said, getting upset. He'd been talking to me less than thirty seconds and I was already lying. "Look, you're fishing for crows in the wind here. Jay's a helluva manager and the only reason I left the Rush was that we disagreed on—we had philosophical differences."

"Like over whether he was sane or not."

"Hey," I said. "Jay Bates is an extremely sound baseball man. If Pat and I have another boy we'll name him after Jay. Get the hell *away* from me, will ya?"

"Just between us," Ron said, "Jay's walked off the pier a few times, hasn't he?"

"He's three games out with an *expansion* team, Ron. What difference does it make if the water runs down his chin when he takes a drink? We're all a little nuts right now, it's been a long haul."

"Did you know he told *USA Today* that you were a bad influence on the Rush when you were there?"

"You guys *always do that!*" I said. I was sore. "You're always running back and forth telling Guy Two that Guy One said he's a choke, and then Guy Two says, 'Oh, yeah? Well, then he's dog puke.' So you go back to Guy One and say, 'Simpson says you're dog puke. Care to respond?' You're like those people who drop lit cigarettes in the woods."

"I think you're overreacting to a relative who's trying to do his job," said Ron, going stiff on me.

"Well, at least I told you direct," I said. I was clocking mighty high on the Righteous Meter and Ron got put off and wouldn't talk to me anymore for a while. But jeez, we had a full load of past history going into those last two weeks; we didn't need any extra thrown in by the crack reporter from the *Daily Paper Hat.* And I didn't know if Jay was crazy or not anyway. The only thing I could say with confidence was that if everybody I knew was a rubber band, Jay would be stretched the farthest.

The reporters also had Davy surrounded, when he might better have used his time finding a spare part for our pitching machine that wouldn't fly off when he started it up. Davy was making a point, as usual, of acting as though everything was smooth and creamy whether it was or not. I think at times he might've liked to let go of his composure and buzz around the clubhouse like an untied balloon, but he didn't do it.

Before that same game in Chicago, in Davy's office, a TV sports guy asked him about the "feud" between him and Jay. "It's a feud of long standing, isn't it?" the guy said. "It's no secret that Bates dislikes you intensely."

Davy had been eating a sandwich at his desk and now he looked up. "Did he say that to you?" he asked curiously.

"Did he say, 'I dislike Tremayne intensely'? Doesn't sound like him, somehow."

"Well, he won't talk to me at all," admitted the sportscaster.

"Now see? There ya go," said Davy. "It's hard to tell what Jay's thinking if he won't say. I can't tell if he dislikes me intensely or not—he hasn't spoken to me since we were both nineteen years old."

After the reporter left, Davy said to me, "Y'know, I'm gettin' a little tired of these guys. They never used to bother me, but now they're all like Oprah. They don't care if I can still get around on a fastball—they want to know if my divorce has affected my concentration. They want to know if the Rush has an emotional advantage being the underdog. Next thing they'll ask if I got titty longer than Jay as a baby. I think baseball's gotten too dull for 'em."

As it was, Davy's hands were getting full trying to keep our hitters and pitchers from going at each other's throats. The regulars were getting cranky because they thought we'd've clinched the division by now with any kind of decent pitching, and the pitchers were miffed because the regulars were telling them about it.

Fabian Koonce started that Friday game in Chicago and wasn't the answer; he got rocked. We lost and the Rush won out West and cut our lead to two games. So the next day when we were boarding the bus at the hotel to go to Wrigley, Ray Kazanski wouldn't let Fabian get on. He stood on the steps in front of the kid and told him he'd have to run alongside and sweat off some of his fat.

When a ballclub isn't playing quite up to snuff, there's a little informal ceremony that goes on called The Placing of the Blame. I suppose that happens in companies in business too; when the profits aren't what they should be all the executives look for somebody to focus the heat on. Maybe Krepley in Processing didn't input the Belson file in time. And then pretty soon poor Krepley isn't invited to the communications meeting.

Somehow Fabian Koonce seemed to invite blame, wherever he went. He wasn't the only pitcher who was getting shelled but he was the most recent, and he was a busher, so Kazanski picked him to lean on. Fabian just stood on the sidewalk, blinking up at Ray, while the pitchers who were already on the bus commenced yelling at Kazanski to shut up and sit his ass down and let the kid aboard.

Kazanski had been partly kidding, but when the pitchers started hollering at him he got stubborn about it. Then some of the other regulars began yelling at the pitchers and it was all building nicely when Davy got up out of his seat and walked to the front of the bus where Kazanski was.

"You running the club now, Ray?" Davy asked him.

Kazanski got sulky. "Way some o' these guys been goin' they don't deserve seats," he muttered.

Davy grinned at him. "Hey, you're a first baseman, Ray, not the traveling secretary. All you gotta do is take your four swings and keep your foot on the goddamn bag, it's a great life."

Kazanski stared at Davy for a moment or two and then brushed past him up the aisle to his seat. Davy waved

Fabian up onto the bus and looked us all over until it got quiet.

"I always figured the guy who's needed least on a ballclub," he said, "is the one who comes up to you after the game and says 'You fucked up' when you already know.

"But if you want it that way we can have a new system. Every time we lose we'll pick the Prime Fuck-Up for that game and he can sit in front of his locker afterward while everybody else walks by and pees on him. We can make it a daily procedure, way we're goin'. See if we can get some fun outta losing."

Nobody seemed to want to vote on that, so we went on to the ballpark. We won that day, the Rush lost and we got our three-game lead back. I told Davy later that I thought he'd handled the situation pretty well. He shrugged and said, "That wasn't me—that was Chance Masterson, Frontier Deppity, handles the lynch mobs when they want to string up the half-breed."

16

THERE ARE ALL KINDS OF PRESSURE, OF COURSE, and the pressure of a close divisional baseball race might strike people as being a pretty mild kind. Pat likes to tell me that baseball has nothing to do with heaven, hell or the homeless, so I shouldn't get worked up over it. But the way I look at it, the *kind* of pressure doesn't matter. Whatever you choose to get tense about, that'll do, and the fact that an outsider doesn't think it's important won't really lessen it any.

I get so tired of hearing about how major leaguers play "a kid's game" for money, as if it's a carefree lark. People who say that have apparently forgotten that kid's games are *tough*. I once gave way a bit under kid's-game pressure—well, not a bit; I buckled completely—so I know what I'm talking about. I *remember*.

When I was in the sixth grade I was a pretty good speller—one of the eight best spellers in my class, as handicapped by my teacher. And one afternoon the eight of us got stood up in front of the rest of the Oak Elementary School student body to determine a champion in a spelling bee in the school gym.

167

Now I thought I'd do all right in this event—no worse than third. I didn't expect to be nervous. It wasn't as though the audience was made up of parents; almost the entire crowd was first-through-fifth-graders who were there to be dazzled by our expertise. I'd done well in the exhibition contests leading up to the match and I figured that as long as they didn't hand me a word with five silent letters in it I might even give Claudia Wolfmeyer, the favorite, a run for her money.

Well, it was the damnedest thing. I was third in the lineup in the first round, and when I went center stage to be given my word I was keyed up, but ready, you know? Well-rested, fit. And the word that the moderator or emcee gave me was "August"—a word so easy that I was embarrassed at my luck.

I still don't know exactly what happened. Some spastic slip-up between my brain and my throat, I guess. I stood up there straight and tall and declared, "August. Capital A-o—"

Well, I knew as I said it that *that* wasn't right. My face caught fire and I gulped and made an immediate stiff left-face and walked off the stage, out of the gym, down the hall and back to my empty classroom, where I sat with my head down listening to my desk until the rest of the sixth-graders got back. One of them, David Gleason, unanimously agreed to be the most backward student in Missouri, was just delighted. He had a kind of guffaw instead of a laugh, and he treated me to it while he repeated, "He thinks August got a 'O' in it!" Somebody must have explained to him that it didn't. The teacher finally told him to leave the poor little choke alone—not in those exact words, but that was the idea. And that was the day I decided not to go into spelling bees as a profession.

I think the source of the pressure that ballplayers and other entertainers feel in key situations is not so much the fear of losing or missing by a little, but the fear of totally crumbling and humiliating themselves. They tell themselves to just let their bodies do what they know how to do, but *I* know that sometimes your body can turn on you—or at least your mouth can.

Of course, as the season went into its final week we still had a good chance of avoiding a major confrontation. For the last month Jay Bates had been staring ahead to the three-game series in California at season's end that would decide the race in a showdown. But all St. Louis needed was to take a four-game lead into that series and none of the games would matter.

By Saturday, September 27, we were home against L.A. for two and the Rush was playing in Santa Rita against San Francisco. We were up by three with five games to go. If we won both our games and the Rush lost one, it was over. What aggravated Davy Tremayne— and me, too—was that nobody outside St. Louis seemed to believe that was going to happen. All the other fans in America just assumed we'd wind up facing off in California because it was "fitting." Those of us who considered it more fitting for St. Louis to slide into the title without fuss were in the minority.

We won on Saturday, beating L.A. 7–3; Davy pitched an old Latin junkballer named Orlando Monzant who we'd picked up after he got released by Pittsburgh, and he got through seven innings before twisting his ankle fielding a bunt. The trainer said he was iffy for the rest of the season, but we didn't need to get much farther. A loss by the Rush on the West Coast would clinch a tie for us.

That night I waited in my room to hear the results of the Rush game and watched *Penny Serenade* with Cary Grant and Irene Dunne on television. They had problems galore in that one. I was sitting in bed crying after their first child died when the station's sports anchor came on and said the Rush had won 3–2, behind Ron Amalfimatanio. We were still three up with four to go.

I called Pat up to snivel about it. "Why can't we have a nice dull finish where we win tomorrow and they lose?" I asked.

"There's a Chinese curse," she said. "It says, 'May you live in interesting times.' Maybe you're cursed."

"There's a Jay Bates curse too," I said. "It goes, 'May you come to California with the season on the line, asshole.' "

"Just remember when you go," she said, "that baseball is not life."

"It *feels* like life," I said. "It's got bosses and workers and paychecks and rules. The only difference—"

"The only difference," she said gently, "is that it doesn't *mean* anything."

"I was gonna say," I said firmly, "that the difference is that in baseball you get a *result*. In life, you can get to your deathbed and look back on what you did and maybe not even be able to figure out whether you finished over .500 or not. In baseball, when the season's over somebody sure enough won and everybody else lost."

"And you want to win tomorrow," she said, "and let everybody else down. Take all the fun out of things."

"I don't want interesting times, I'll tell you that," I said.

Davy was really strapped for pitchers on Sunday. Lefty Smith was off the DL but his arm was still suspect and we didn't want to use him unless we had to, out West. It wasn't Seeburger's turn yet. Briggs was in the bullpen trying to find the plate. Monzant had just pitched and was hurt anyway.

So Davy went with our marginal kids, and they couldn't do it, was all. L.A. just beat hell out of us. For that game it looked like *they* belonged in first place and we belonged in the litterbox.

Davy started one bum, and when that bum got clobbered he replaced him with another, and then he replaced that one with Fabian Koonce, by which time we were already down 8–0. Fabian came in and got a double play on a line drive that he caught behind his back by accident, and that was the only thing we did right all day.

It was our last home game of the year and the fans had come out all pumped up to see us maybe clinch the title, but they got the idea early that it wasn't going to happen and sat quiet, looking into the distance, shelling their peanuts. They didn't boo. It was more like somebody had died earlier in the day and they were observing two-and-a-half hours of silence. The Rush beat San Francisco that night so we took a two-game lead to Santa Rita.

I sat next to Davy on the plane to California Monday. He had a sheet of paper on which he was writing his pitching options for the series. When he was done, just before he crumpled it up, it looked like this:

> Seeburger—Big deal.
> Lefty Smith—Can he throw?
> Monzant—Can he walk?
> Briggs—Can he throw without walks?

Next to this last question, Davy had drawn an approximation of the Santa Rita diamond with Briggs on the mound, firing a fastball up into the press box.

When Davy had balled up his note he said, "I hate my pitchers. What do you think would happen if I pitched myself, as one of the Never-Land All-Stars? Jack Telvley, maybe?"

"Mutiny," I said. He nodded solemnly and stared out the window.

We got into the airport in the late afternoon. When we were getting our bags I noticed a father and his young son looking at us. The daddy had a Rush jacket on. So did the little boy, who I gauged to be about five. The kid walked up to me, came up to mid-thigh, looked up and said, "Are you with St. Louis?"

I said yeah.

"Boo," said the kid.

You know, for years everybody's been saying that Southern Californians are "laid-back" people who just skateboard and surf and leave the ballpark in the seventh inning, but the majority of the ones I've seen don't fit the profile.

For one thing there's so many of them now, and they all get stuck on the freeway and red in the face. Drive around out there for a while and then tell me how laidback everybody is.

And the Rush fans were not the kind to doze off or get more interested in a beachball in the stands than the game on the field. They came to the park to make themselves heard while the Rush ran right up the other team's chest. The core group, the Rushians, were loud, proud and rowdy, and they stayed till the end.

What happened, I think, was that Jay's style had influenced the fans as well as his players. Customers who found the established California teams too rich and bland adopted the Rush because the players were young wild men, and there were several hundred thousand other young wild men in the area who could identify with them and their manager.

The personality that set the tone for the Rush was definitely Jay's, not Sunset Boone's. Sunset was kind of a genial ruler at the top of the pile, but he wasn't accessible to the fans because he was a big movie star with a chauffeur. Jay was the representative of every Californian who got in a frenzy and pounded on his steering wheel while he sat on the 405 freeway with the rest of the population wondering why his car didn't have a bathroom in it. These were people who wanted to *get there,* and they had the Rush rhythm instinctively. The Rush played ball the way they all wanted to drive—seventy miles per hour on the shoulder, past everybody who was waiting in line.

And when we got out to Santa Rita for the last three games, we were the only car the Rush and their fans still had to pass before they could floor it down the road to the championship, singing in the breeze.

Of course, we were still ahead, but that didn't carry much weight out West. The first paper I picked up at the airport had a piece on how the Rush was turning Davy Tremayne's hair white. Davy was offended.

"They act like *they're* in first place, like *they* only need to win the first game," he complained. "They think it's *Rocky One.*"

The same writers who had said before the season started that the Rush would be lucky to finish last were now assuring their readers that their team had all the momentum and ours was reeling, with a pitching staff shot to hell and a manager who was aging visibly every minute.

Our pitching *was* looking bad, but the rest of us were healthy, and Davy's tint wasn't going to be crucial to the outcome. What bothered me more about Davy was that he wasn't quite himself—whoever that may have been— coming into California. He'd always been supremely confident, the kind of guy who would let you come back at him in Ping-Pong until you were within a point and then slam one down your throat so you had another Adam's apple. I'd never seen him indicate any concern about the result of a competitive event he was involved in. He'd always been convinced that if he gave his opponent a little of this and a little of that he'd eventually come out the gracious victor.

But coming into the last three games he was slightly different. Not scared or nervous, exactly, but uncomfortable, like his uniform was inside out. If the race had worn Jay Bates down physically until he was mostly bones and fever, it had worked Davy into a corner where he couldn't get full extension for his arms and legs. He didn't like being stuck with the pitchers he had, and his dissatisfaction with them brought out the one quirky trait he'd always had and made it more like a fetish.

You never know how that pressure, when you finally feel it, is going to hit you. In my case, years ago, it made me turn what I knew damn well was a "U" into an "O." In Davy's, it surfaced as a desire to turn his players into Never-Land All-Stars.

17

I WALKED INTO DAVY'S OFFICE IN THE VISITORS' clubhouse two hours before the first game of the series and found him a little fussed. He couldn't stand the idea of starting Howard Seeburger.

Howard was the logical choice—the only choice, really—but Davy just didn't have any confidence in him. And he didn't blame Seeburger's fastball or slider for his ineffectiveness in the last month or so; he blamed his name.

"The guy's name says 'loser,' " he said flatly. "He's spent his whole career with a name that encourages him to be mediocre."

"Shouldn't you be working out the lineup?" I suggested.

"I've *got* the lineup, I *know* the lineup, never *mind* the lineup," said Davy, and looked at a piece of paper he'd been writing on.

"Listen to this," he said after a moment, and began reading names, slowly and impressively: "Whitey Ford. Sandy Koufax. Don Drysdale. Bob Feller. Grover Cleveland Alexander. Cy Young. Juan Marichal. Christy Mathewson. Schoolboy Rowe. Lefty Grove. Satchel Paige. Smoky Joe Wood. Eddie Plank. Chief Bender. Three-Finger

Brown." He looked up and stared at me. "Howard Seeburger."

"Don't you think you're letting—"

"This guy's been living his life under a cloud," said Davy. "A man like that, you put him center stage in the big game and all you'll see after his name in the box score when it's over is 'L.' "

He'd sent for Seeburger, and a minute later the big guy came into the office and Davy told him to sit down. Howard may have expected to hear some shrewd insight about the Rush lineup; I don't know. Or maybe he expected something like what he heard, because he sure reacted quickly enough.

Davy said to him, "When you're out there on the mound tonight, I want you to think of yourself as 'Riverboat Ralston.' "

"Goddamnit, stop *doin'* that!" Seeburger exploded, up on his feet instantly. It was the first time I'd seen him blow up in the short time I'd known him. "Sonofa*bitch,* skip, I got enough to think about without trying to remember if I'm King Kong this or Riverboat something else! What the hell's goin' *on* with you? I'm fuckin' Howie Seeburger and I'm gonna pitch Howie Seeburger's game! I ain't changin' my name for you or anybody else!" He walked out muttering, "Jesus Christ!" and Davy looked at me in a resigned way.

"He'd do better as Jesus Christ than he's gonna do as himself," he said. "You try to help these guys, but they don't understand the game's mental, it's all up here."

Davy seemed to release his brainstorm easily. He crumpled up his page of pitching greats, tossed it in the wastebasket and went out to try to outmanage Jay in a more conventional way.

*   *   *

The park in Santa Rita was kind of cheesy for a major league stadium; Sunset Boone planned on renovating it considerably after the season, adding seats and luxury boxes and so on. It had been a minor league park before he got the franchise and it still looked a little raggedy-ass. Out past the bleachers in the outfield there was nothing but parking lot, and there was no massive scoreboard or RushVision video replay or anything like that. It only held about thirty-eight thousand people. Before the season nobody thought they'd fill it much after Opening Day anyway, but the way things turned out it was jammed to the roof and clogged in the aisles for our series. It was a good pitcher's park, because the playing field itself was large, and good for the fans who could squeeze into it too, because they were pretty close to the field all the way around.

I'd been in there often, and I'd heard the Rushians at a high pitch at times, but nothing like what I heard when we played that series. You could shout to yourself and swear nothing came out.

Howie Seeburger, pitching as Howie Seeburger, really didn't do too badly in game one considering he was standing in the middle of a hysterical mob. I don't know that Riverboat Ralston could've done any better. Howie had a 2–2 tie in the bottom of the sixth against Joe Kaiser, but then Slip Washington slipped going for a ball in the alley with two men on and we were done. Kaiser beat us 4–3 and our lead was cut to one game with two left.

When Kaiser got Garry Perry on a grounder to short for the last out, thirty-eight-thousand-plus people, already on their feet, seemed to rise up higher on lung expansion and let us all have it. We'd certainly brought these fans a lot of happiness. It's so easy to cheer people up on the road; all you have to do is lose. Of course you can't feel too good about it yourself, looking up at a park full of guys in T-shirts with the tendons standing out in their necks, screaming, "Get a job!"

There was one world-class howler behind our dugout who "announced" the whole game at the top of his voice from the beginning for the benefit of his neighbors. He'd consulted his scorecard in the top of the first and bellowed: "The *first* faggot batting for St. Louis is George Washington!" Then he'd gone on from there. If he ever actually got up into the booth he'd have to tone it down considerably, believe me. Davy called him "Lungs."

Jay Bates wasn't really a prominent part of that first game. He was hunched over on the bench in the Rush dugout most of the time, rubbing his hands together constantly like they were cold—the new signs, I figured—and looking very tiny. He never stood up, that I saw, until the end of the game, when he got up slow, bent forward, in the middle of all his players, who were jumping up with their arms in the air and bounding onto the field to hug Kaiser. Jay moved like an old man shuffling through the park, holding himself together with his hands in his pockets. It's tough when you have to win them all.

And it's tough when you only have to win one and can't. Davy was quiet in the clubhouse afterward, looking thoughtful. I didn't disturb him, not wanting to interrupt all the staring off into space a manager has to do between games.

Before the Wednesday night game Lefty Smith came up to Davy in the clubhouse and said, "You don't want this to go on another day, do you?"

"Hell, no," said Davy.

"Let me start," said Smith. "I'll go as far as I can."

Lefty Smith had the kind of stuff the Rush hated—change of speeds on his fastball. He was a "painter," worked the corners, and best of all he was a cold bastard who wouldn't care about things like crowd noise and long leadoffs. He was an excellent poker player, best on the team by yards—one of those icemen, a guy with no lips and a strong stare. He'd draw two and sandbag whoever raised and look at him as if to say, *"You* figure it out." A crowd could yell in Lefty Smith's ear all night and he wouldn't notice.

The only problem was his arm was maybe coming apart. Our team doctor wanted him to have surgery in the off-season, and just because he could now *warm* up without pain didn't mean he could *heat* up without throwing his arm to the plate along with the pitch.

But Davy didn't have much else, and a manager likes it when his ace asks for the ball. So he penciled him in.

There's a limit to how far you can get on guts alone, and Lefty reached it on his third batter of the night. With two out in the bottom of the first he tried to throw a good fastball and we could all tell it was probably over. Lefty turned pretty white out there. He got the ball back from Hartman and walked around the mound, and Davy and the trainer went out to talk to him. When they came back after Smith had lobbed a few practice pitches, Davy told me, "He wants to get one more batter."

Well, the batter was Darrell Paris, sad to say, and to him, Lefty was now like a boxer with his hands down. The next pitch Smith threw was supposed to be another fastball, but it took too long to arrive. Darrell's eyes got big and he stepped into it with his whole body—a beautiful swing, really, if you could stand to watch it. The sound of the bat hitting the ball was heard, it seemed, in complete surrounding silence, and then the fans gasped and exploded. I thought Pat would be able to hear them in Illinois.

Lefty never looked at the ball as it sailed out into the night; he just squatted down at the foot of the mound with his arm in his lap. I knew I'd lose sight of the ball anyway, so I just watched Smith while Paris trotted the bases around him and walked the last twenty feet to the plate to do forearm bashes with Turk and the rest of the Rush. It sure seemed like a lot more than one run. It seemed like the end of the season.

It was the end for Smith, anyway. He came off the field cradling his arm while Lungs yelled, "Amputate!" from his seat behind our dugout, and added, "They're gonna have to call you 'Righty'!"

Davy brought in Todd Briggs because he had the best stuff of the remaining pitchers—a logical move that both Davy and I knew was wrong anyway. There was no way a kid like Briggs was going to close off the Rush in a spot like that. He got to warm up as long as he wanted but after that we had to play, and it seemed like the game lasted till dawn.

The kid did his best, but he was behind everybody. He walked a few and he couldn't hold them; they all stole on his high leg kick. Briggs got a lot of strikeouts, but the Rush got about a run per inning anyway. We lost. We lost by plenty. And when the game finally ended, the edge St. Louis had had all year was gone.

I had all the time I could want to look around after the score got lopsided and I spent most of it watching Jay, who was right near me there in the Rush dugout when I was in the third-base coach's box. He never, at any time, looked like he was happy or had the game won. He didn't say anything. For him it was a nailbiter until the last out. Then he slumped back on the bench and closed his eyes.

Davy and I stayed in our dugout for a few minutes when it was over and watched the Rushians celebrate.

"You know, I never did that," said Davy. "I never jumped up and down and hugged strangers over *anything*. They all look like they just found out they're going to heaven: no slip-ups, no twist at the last minute—they're *going*."

Lungs waved at us merrily with one hand and pretended to strangle himself with the other, a well-known kind of sports sign language.

The next day, a few hours before the Last Game, a photographer from *The Sporting News* came up to me and said he wanted to get a group picture of Jay Bates, Davy Tremayne and Charlie Tyke: "The three guys from Monmouth in the big one together."

"Good luck," I told him.

"You don't want to do it?"

I shrugged. "I don't think you can get Jay and Davy to agree to it. But if they will I will."

To my surprise, they did it. I've got that picture in front of me now. I'm in the middle, because the photographer thought it was balanced that way—the antagonists on either side and the guy from both teams in between.

When we met in front of the batting cage, Jay looked as though he hadn't been taking his medication. If that lad had slept in the last three nights I'm Niff Naffner. But I wouldn't say he was tired; he was several months past tired. He looked eager. His eyes were red and huge and it seemed like he'd forgotten how to blink them; they were Open 24 Hours.

It was his big evening. Looking back, it occurred to me that Davy's statement about Jay not speaking to him since Monmouth was correct; I could recall a couple times when Davy had spoken to *Jay,* but there'd been no response. Tonight, though, they were finally on even ground.

Davy was in a weird mood. I'd seen him in the clubhouse before we went onto the field and expected him to be ramming his fingers through his gray hair some, but he looked serene and satisfied, like he'd come to a decision about something.

The photographer asked him if he'd named a starting pitcher for the big game and Davy said no.

Jay ran his teeth over his lower lip a couple times and said, "He ain't got one."

"Afternoon, Jay," said Davy easily. "Sleep well?"

Jay said, "I'll sleep tonight."

"Glad to know we're speaking," said Davy. "I want you boys to give us a good game, Jay. If it's a good one you and I can do some commercials together, whaddya say?"

"Tell ya something," said Jay, and came over near us to talk confidentially and conversationally. "All these years, you always had the edge on me, but tonight's different. It's my yard, my game and my turn. I got my ace workin' and I don't care who you throw, we'll run him outta here. Your balls are in the vise." Jay looked at me and showed his teeth. "And your boyfriend Tyke here was right, it's better to beat ya than kill ya. The birds are singin' in the trees. There ain't been a minute in your whole fuckin' life when you've been as happy as I'm gonna be tonight. They're gonna shit on your picture in St. Louis."

The photographer moved us into position while Davy murmured, "And they say he dislikes me intensely."

We were asked to smile into the camera, which Jay thought was a funny request, showing ignorance of our history. He snickered and said to me, "He thinks we're the Three Mouseketeers."

And damned if the guy didn't get his smiles, in a way. I'm looking at the picture here before me. Davy hadn't grinned much since we got to California, but there's the Tremayne smile, right into the lens, saying, "Isn't it great to be me?" And Jay—Jay has a gap-toothed grin and a gleam in his eyes I don't recall ever seeing, as if he was a mad scientist who'd just invented the liquid chemical that could blow up everybody in the world except him and his slave girls. I'm the only one whose smile looks phony. I look sort of like a hostage.

I'M SURE THAT IN THE REST OF THE WORLD ON
that evening of the Last Game, people were going about
their business, having babies and surgery and policing
their area, but in Santa Rita there was only one show and
one subject. That rickety old ballpark was surrounded
hours before game time, and inside it the media guys
were elbowing each other in the teeth trying to get at Jay
and Davy and the players.

It made me realize how tough a job those guys have,
fighting to get a few words for themselves. Players like
Darrell Paris and Lefty Smith don't make for an easy
interview at the best of times; they consider the press to
be jackals or flies. In this kind of situation, the man with
the mike has to muscle in like a broker at the commodi-
ties exchange in Chicago, frantic to get somebody's attention. And then like as not the athlete will tell him to go
fuck himself.

Our locker room was not festive. One of the players, I
think Hurricane Hartman, had yelled at the clubhouse
man to get rid of the victory champagne we'd had sitting
around for the two previous games because it was a jinx.

The guys all looked like I must've at my sixth-grade spelling bee—a little grim.

Easily the loosest man in our corner was Davy Tremayne. I found him in his office a little while after the photo session, sitting at his desk, reading all the papers.

"Why don't you sit down for an hour or so?" he said. "You look worried about something."

"I'm not if you're not," I said, sitting.

"How does everybody else look?"

"Like they got sore throats."

"You know, it's a funny thing," said Davy. "I don't think there's a story in all these papers that doesn't have the word 'choke' in it somewhere. Used to be these guys had to think twice about their health before they employed that term, but now they all do it."

"Well, they think we're in the process of blowing a putt that looked pretty short a week ago."

"You know the mistake I made?" Davy asked me, leaning forward, serious, looking surprised to find he could've made one. "I got to thinking like a regular person. I've been managing like a regular person all this while. I forgot what got me here. I was acting like Davy Tremayne, and Davy Tremayne is the one guy who could've lost this thing." He leaned back and shook his head, marveling at his own foolishness.

"So who are you now?" I asked. "Bat Belfry?"

"Good one, Charlie," he said. "But I'm using the full resources of my imagination again. The best guys I've ever been. Adapt your identity to the demands of the moment, that's the key. You've seen the last of Tremayne."

"Swell," I said, "but the guys out there are still who *they* are, and right now they're thinking that may not be good enough."

"They'll be all right. I was just worried about who to pitch, and now I know, I've got it. I was thinking all night about this guy and that guy, Monzant, even Seeburger."

"Monzant's still wobbly," I said. "Seeburger might not be bad, he's got a rubber arm."

"Seeburger would pitch just well enough to lose," said Davy. "I want somebody who'll jump off the page when they write about this game all down through time. The one guy who fits the situation. Who's Jay pitching? Ron Amalfimatanio. Is that the winner of a game for the ages?"

"He's the winner of nineteen games this year."

"He won't get the twentieth. Ron Amalfimatanio will not live in legend and lore. They won't write a five-verse rap song about Amalfimatanio. He'll lose, Charlie. He'll lose to Fabian Koonce."

Somehow I'd known he was going to say that, but it didn't make it any easier to take.

"Davy, I like the kid but he's the worst pitcher we've got left."

"He won't be today," said Davy. "Today he's going to make the history his parents meant for him to make when they said to each other, 'Our boy ain't gonna be just another Koonce.' " Davy got up and walked around his desk to sit against it and convince me. " 'We'll name him Fabian,' they said. 'Not Homer or Jethro— Fabian.' You know in your heart, Charlie, that when that boy's mother gave him that name, her eyes *shone*. It was *special*."

Well, it made me sad. It was disillusioning after all these years to find out that when push came to shove, Davy Tremayne could walk right up to Jay Bates on equal terms, put his finger to his lips and say, "Bllbllbllbllbllbllblblbllll." It was a little scary, too, like in those movies where the brilliant psychiatrist turns out to be the homicidal maniac.

For a moment it made me wonder about myself. First I'd worked for Jay and thought he might be over the precipice, and now I was feeling the same way about Davy. When you think that about too many people you'd better consider the possibility that it ain't them, it's you.

But for Christ's sake, Fabian Koonce? With his 8.43 ERA and his blank expression and his goggles? In the biggest game in years? It wasn't even *trying*. It was more like if you were in the middle of the road and a truck was bearing down on you, and instead of sidestepping it you did a card trick. It was clear to me that Davy had found reality unbearable and was just ignoring it.

I said, "I hope you won't be offended if I say that, one, Fabian Koonce's name isn't all that great, and two, even talking about it is making me feel like tying you down."

"Okay, forget the name," said Davy. "I'm always willing to pretend I'm rational. He doesn't walk anybody, does he? They'll have to hit him, won't they? And he doesn't get nervous either. You ever see him nervous?"

"No," I admitted. "I guess he could take a beating without flinching. He's done it often enough."

"Bring him in here, I want to talk to him," said Davy.

So, just as I'd gone to get Fabian so Jay could talk to him at the beginning of the season, I went to get him

188

so Davy could talk to him at the end. He came in with just his jock on again, all solemn and bewildered in his glasses.

"Son, go back out there and put some clothes on," said Davy. "It wasn't that urgent." Koonce left and Davy said to me, "When I see him like that I start to lose confidence."

Fabian returned in his uniform pants and T-shirt a few minutes later and Davy asked him to sit down.

"Fabian," Davy said, "do you think you can get the ball over the plate in the middle of that din out there?"

"Yessir," said Koonce, blinking slowly.

"Do you believe you were born to greatness?"

Fabian thought that one over longer. "I never considered it."

"Never mind," said Davy. "I'm thrusting greatness on you. Few men have had the chance I'm giving you today, Fabian. I believe that of all the guys at my disposal, you're the one who can go out there and grab fortune by the stones. When this day is over you'll be a famous name in baseball history. Kids all over the country are gonna put your baseball card in little plastic pockets."

"They don't have a card of me, skip," said Koonce.

"That's because they can't *see,* they don't have any vision," said Davy. "Next year your card will start at three-fifty. You're going to win the big one. You'll be on *Letterman* and *Saturday Night Live.* They'll ask you what you eat for breakfast. What do you eat for breakfast?"

"Eggs."

"Farm fresh?"

"When I'm home."

"Let me suggest a name-brand cereal to go with those eggs," said Davy. "Glory days don't last forever. Leave no endorsement stone unturned."

Fabian had lost the thread of the conversation; he looked like he was watching a loved one leave on the train. "I'm sorry, skip, but I can't figure out what you're talkin' about," he said.

"I'll be straightforward," said Davy. "You're starting. You've got the ball."

Fabian looked from Davy to me to the wall and started nodding deliberately. "Well, that's fine," he said finally.

"Prospect doesn't put any fright into you?" Davy asked.

"Not right this minute," said Koonce. "But I'm still not clear in my mind on why I'm your choice."

"You don't think it's logical," said Davy. "Well, in the last few weeks, Fabian, logic has lost me a six-game lead. The guy on the other side of the field beats logic like a drum. Tonight I'm gonna let him look at you instead. You have no great admiration for Jay Bates, do you?"

"It ain't my way to talk people down, but in my view he's the only kind of worm that's bad for the soil."

"You're gonna make a great interview, son," said Davy. "Now I want you to go find Hurricane and talk over the hitters with him. Keep in mind that you're destiny's child tonight, Fabian. You're going out there a hayseed and coming back a star."

Our catcher, Hartman, came into the office a few minutes later more like a hurricane than I would have thought possible. He said a few thousand words to the effect that Davy was handing the title to the Rush and that Koonce couldn't get through the national anthem without getting line drives hit at him. Davy just sat back and let him go on till he was done, and then said, "Is this mutiny, Hartman? I was warned of this."

With Fabian he'd been like Warner Baxter in an old Broadway picture and now he was talking to Hartman like Captain Bligh. It was getting crowded in his office, sitting there with a cavalcade of characters, so I went out to the locker room to get myself ready for the game.

After infield and batting practice Davy got the guys together in the locker room to say a few words. Fabian was down in the pen warming up. By this time everybody knew Koonce was starting and they ranged in attitude from stricken to pissed. Davy was cheerful.

"Koonce tells me he can get the ball over the plate, gentlemen," he said. "And that makes your job pretty simple. We're gonna concentrate on fundamentals. You boys have fun and I'll take care of da mentals." Davy laughed happily during the silence that followed this remark. Taylor Cheney, our pitching coach, was sitting next to me and I heard him mutter, "Oh, *no.*"

"Now Hurricane, here," Davy went on, "*he* tells me he lacks confidence in my choice of starter for this game. He says if I think we're going to win behind Koonce I'm full of shit. Well, boys, let me tell you something." Davy paused impressively, and then said with authority: "I *am* full of shit. That shit has gotten me where I am today. You'll never get anywhere in life if you can't shit yourself that you're better than you are. If I've failed you anywhere along the line in the last week it's because I haven't lied to you enough, but I'm putting that right, right now. We're gonna win this game."

191

He certainly had everyone's attention. I don't know
when I've ever heard a pep talk that had such a contradic-
tory conviction to it.

"If you don't believe you can win it for yourselves,"
said Davy now, with some passion, "believe you can win
it for me. Because I believe our worst can beat their
best. Because I believe in the power of the human mind
to overcome the truth. If you can't win, change into
someone who can. Lie to yourselves, boys . . . and win
this one for the Shitter."

Some years back—I think in Cleveland, but I won't raise
my right hand to say so—the management of the home
ballclub, desperate to goose the attendance, hit upon a
promotion that turned into one of the all-time boomerang
ideas: Ten-Cent Beer Night. For some reason, when
they were dreaming this idea up nobody speculated much
on what a baseball crowd might be like after two or three
hours of bargain drinking. By the end of the game both
teams were pulling fans out of their hair and that particular promotion was discontinued.

I wasn't present on that occasion, but lively as it must
have been I don't see how that crowd could have been
any more energetic than ours was on the night of the
Last Game between St. Louis and the Rush. And the
Santa Rita fans started *out* uplifted, even though they
were paying for their beer in the old-fashioned ballpark
way—through the nose.

Sunset Boone was happy as game time approached,
sitting with Jessup in the boxes behind the third-base

dugout, waving his pearl-gray cowboy hat at everybody and counting the house. For contrast, Fabian Koonce was back in our locker room throwing up.

I found that out when Hurricane Hartman brought me to see the kid, I guess because I was known to have had a longer relationship with Koonce than anybody else on the club. "He puked right there on the floor, I'm tellin' ya," Hartman said. Well, several guys have done that before a big game, but Hurricane and I went back into the clubhouse anyway to see what we could do.

Fabian was sitting in front of his locker, watching the clubhouse man clean up his midday meal.

"Somethin' go down wrong, kid?" I asked him.

"I been thinkin' about how all the players say I stink," he said. "Makes me feel like they don't have any faith in me."

I looked at Hartman, who cleared his throat and said, "Hell, Koonce, all you gotta worry about is the Rush. Never mind what *we* think."

Fabian took a deep breath after those encouraging words and looked at me, with his mouth hanging open. I couldn't picture him on the *Letterman* show.

"Maybe this'll help a little," I said. "Those guys are taking big leads off the bases. When they get on, Fabe, you give 'em a couple crappy moves to first, let 'em get out there as far as they want. Then *you*"—I said to Hartman—"try to pick 'em off. They may be overextending tonight. You might get somebody cheap. But you'll have to gun it over there. Don't get up, just throw out of your crouch."

"Coaches," said Hartman to Koonce. "Do this, do that. C'mon, Country. You got nothin' left to lose, here, it's all on the floor."

Jay Bates didn't believe that Fabian was going to start for us. When he saw him warming up before the game he assumed it was a trick of some kind and that maybe the real pitcher was in our locker room practicing the shot put. Jay came over to our dugout at one point to say, "Tremayne, your jokes weren't funny in Monmouth and they're not funny now."

But when Davy sent me up to the plate with his lineup and Jay and the umps got a look at Koonce's name on it, Jay had to accept it as official. He said to me, "The mother's done it this time. He's gone too far. That's not confidence, it's crazy. He's lost his fuckin' mind."

"Maybe he knows something," I said, although I couldn't imagine what.

"He's livin' in a dream world," Jay said flatly.

"No, he's not," I said with dignity. "He's living in a fool's paradise."

"I'm tellin' ya up front," said Jay, raising his voice as we separated and went back to our dugouts, "don't send Koonce out there. We'll run that farm boy's sorry ass back to the shit patch! You think you can beat us with *nothin'?* It's comin' outta your *ears,* Tyke!"

Seeing Jay in such high pregame spirits added to those of the crowd. Lungs, behind our dugout again, was in excellent voice. When the Rush took the field for the top of the first after the lineups had been announced, Lungs led the cheers. He hollered "*GOOM-*

BA!" at Ron Amalfimatanio about thirty times before Ronnie finished his warm-ups, and the rest of the time he was yelling, "You're a genius, Jay! The man with the plan! Hey, Tremayne! Hey, Wrong-Way! You pitch Koonce and they'll suspend you for life! You're throwin' the title, buddy! You're sellin' it! Here's *my* dollar! Run that fat boy out there and this bill is *yours!*" and so on.

When I got over to the third-base box I found Jay much peppier than he'd been the first two games.

"Tyke," he yelled, for the benefit of the other guys on his bench, "if you pitch Koonce it's an *in*sult, you hear me? That's the same lardass couldn't get anybody out for us! Tremayne's a dead done deal! It's gonna be so easy it's pissin' me off! Hey, Charlie! Hey! Hey, Tyke! Hey! Hey, Charlie!"

I finally got exasperated and turned around and said, "*What?*"

Jay looked aggrieved all of a sudden. "He's not *really* gonna pitch that kid, is he?" he asked.

Well, hell. It looked that way. After the anthem I took a look at the crowd while the Rush infielders threw the ball around and Ronnie Amalfimatanio got set to pitch to George Washington, and I said to myself, "*Remember* this," like you do sometimes when you're living through a minute that's going to stand out from the millions that slip away in your life. I was lucky tonight, in spite of the likelihood that my ballclub was going to get tromped. Most seasons don't come down to the last day, and even the ones that do usually find me on the couch, watching from a distance like any other fan. But I hadn't been cheated this time. This was a game they were going to remember, and I was Charlie Tyke on the spot, in uniform. I even had to pee again, like before my first game in the majors. It goes away when the game starts.

19

JAY'S RUSH LINEUP WAS EXACTLY THE SAME AS it had been on Opening Day: Shain-Biela-Paris-Turk-Fanzone-Surface-Gonder-Miranda-Amalfimatanio. Davy's read like this:

> George Washington, CF
> Garry Perry, SS
> Dave Tremayne, 2B
> John Casale, LF
> Ray Kazanski, 1B
> Hector Herrera, RF
> Ted Grim, 3B
> Hurricane Hartman, C
> Fabian Koonce, P

In the top of the first our hitters looked as confused by Ron Amalfimatanio's stuff as they'd been by Davy's pregame talk; even Davy himself was flailing. We went down one-two-three, and the crowd kicked up the volume with each out. Jay was alive in the Rush dugout, yanking his fist back and forth through the air whenever

Ronnie retired someone. Jay's body English was that of a man delivering hundreds of rapid-fire punches to somebody's midsection. When Davy popped up for the third out, Jay finished with a right uppercut to the sky and then crouched at the end of the home dugout, waiting to see if Koonce was really, truly going to walk out to the mound for us.

When Fabian shambled out to the center of the diamond, Jay was a study. He looked the way you would if a stranger came up to you on the street and tried to hand you a hundred-dollar bill. He looked askance, I would say. He tilted his head like dogs do when they're trying extra hard to understand you, and squinted for a long time at Davy, who was taking grounders at second.

Davy himself didn't look like a dead done deal; he didn't seem to know he was playing posthumously. He had some salt in his hair and an extra few pounds but other than that he was the Can't-Miss Kid from Monmouth as far as I could see.

Fabian Koonce looked like he always did out there—misplaced. Big, lumpy, mouth open, staring through his glasses at Hartman, he was the least athletic-looking guy on the field. Watching him, I wondered if he had his best stuff, and whether it mattered.

When Fabian had his stuff, such as it was, he had that wrinkly slider and a curve that bent down as it reached the plate, mostly because it lost momentum. His fastball was only fast in comparison with his other pitches, which wouldn't have been a bad thing except that it was straight, with no hop, no veer, no sail, no verve. He'd reached the majors on control, and maybe on appearance—he looked so big and goony out there that I think sometimes hitters got distracted staring at him and popped up his slider.

Odd as he looked, Fabian *was* coordinated. His motion on the first pitch was nice and smooth and easy, and so was the pitch, and J. W. Shain, batting lefty, smoked it to right for a single.

On Fabian's first serve to Tony Biela, J.W. took off. Tony hit a hard fly to right center that ordinarily would have been caught by either Slip Washington or Hector Herrera, but the crowd noise was so strong that neither of them heard the other one calling for it.

J.W. had to protect himself from being doubled up and was hustling back toward first as our two outfielders both got there in time to make the catch—which was their misfortune. The ball landed on their gloves and seemed to blow them apart like a bomb. It hit the ground about the same time they did.

Shain, running backward, and Biela, running forward, were within a few feet of each other near first when the ball dropped, so they started going around the bases together, Biela just a couple steps behind Shain. Davy Tremayne ran out past the outfielders to chase down the ball.

When J.W. and Biela got to third, Jay's coach, Leo Keeler, did what I think I would've done: He waved Shain toward home with his right hand and held up his left for Biela to stop. But two things went wrong with that tactic. First J.W., whose super-speed wasn't what it had been in June, stumbled going by Leo and lost some steam, and second, Tony Biela ignored Keeler's stop sign completely and ran up Shain's back. I guess Tony had gotten it so firmly drummed into his head that you went *forward* on the Rush that the idea of holding up was no longer part of his philosophy.

Biela knocked J.W. forward and the two of them staggered home, where Hartman was waiting with the ball, which had come from Davy to Kazanski to the plate. Hurricane tagged them out one after the other for a double play. I don't know how you'd score it—8-9-4-3-2-to-the-second-power, or something.

While the fans were summing that one up for each other, we checked on Slip Washington and Herrera. Washington was okay but Hector had to come out with a banged-up knee. Davy put our fourth outfielder, Dan Keaton, in right. Fabian had only thrown two pitches and it already looked like the circus was in town.

When we resumed, Paris and Turk singled hard, and Fanzone beat out a smash off Teddy Grim's glove at third for another hit to load the bases. Then Joe Surface lined one so solidly off Fabian's stomach that it rolled all the way back to Hartman, who threw Surface out. The Rush had gotten five hits in the inning but hadn't scored.

With the bases loaded and the crowd at full holler, Davy had gone to the mound and yelled something in Fabian's ear. Between innings I asked Davy what he'd said.

"I told him to get his glove up so he wouldn't stop one with his face, and then they hit him in the belly," said Davy, grinning. "Wow! Five hits and nothin'! Look at Jay!"

Jay was stomping around the Rush dugout flamenco style, whipping his head around and spitting out three "fucks" a second, like the old locomotive football cheer: "BOOM-fucka-fucka-fucka, BOOM-fucka-fucka-fucka."

Hartman came up to Davy and said, "You gonna get somebody up in the pen or what?"

"Why?" said Davy.

"*Why?*" Hartman exploded. "Because he didn't get anybody *out,* that's why!"

"He got the last guy out, Hurricane," said Davy. "I'll admit he didn't fool 'em out there, but look how he teased the crowd. Kid's a born showman."

Hartman said, "You *are* the Shitter, aren't ya?" and walked away. Davy said to me, "Actually I was lying when I said I was a shitter. Guy's got a point, though—I thought Fabian would do better. I'll yank him when they start to score." He went and talked to Taylor Cheney and a few minutes later I saw Monzant and Seeburger cranking up down the line.

Amalfimatanio had a good, rising fastball. He ran his heat right by us in the top of the second, fanning Casale and popping up Kazanski and Keaton. We were out on six pitches. As I walked away from third base and Fabian took the mound, rubbing his belly a little, I heard Jay behind me, clapping his hands and yelling, "He won't get through another inning. Fuckin' God won't let it happen."

Jay was in a sweat to get to Koonce before Davy regained his senses and took him out, so he had the Rush hitters swinging from the get-go. Tom Gonder led off the bottom of the inning with a single and Jay had him running on the first pitch to Marty Miranda, but Fabian pitched out and Gonder got nailed by ten feet. Then Marty singled to center, and when *he* broke for second on the next pitch

Hartman got him too—or at least the ump said he did. Davy did one of his matador sweeps on the tag and threw up some dust and Marty got called out. He could've beefed about it, but Miranda always believed he had the right to remain silent, so he just rose and trotted off the field while Jay charged out of his dugout to crawl all over the ump.

Davy told me after the inning that the main point Jay stressed to Vern Rennick, the second-base umpire, was that ballet and baseball were different.

"This *dancer*," Jay had yelled, indicating Davy, "has been doin' that goddamn sweep for twenty years and you guys just think it's got syrup on it, you think it's so fuckin' pretty. But the *rules* say if he's late with the tag it doesn't *matter* if it's pretty, and he was *LATE!*"

Rennick said, "Your guy didn't bitch about it."

"My guy can't *talk!*" screamed Jay. "All he knows is Bueno! You're supposed to call the *play*, you're not supposed to listen for the fuckin' echo!"

"I called the play," said Rennick. "He's out."

There was more, but that was the basic platform of each party. Jay's was the popular view but Miranda was out anyway.

With two down Amalfimatanio singled, and when J. W. Shain lined one over third for extra bases I thought Ronnie was a sure thing to score. But as the ball was about to carom off the face of the left-field boxes, a fan reached over and caught it. So it was a dead ball and a ground-rule double and Amalfimatanio had to go back to third.

The crowd just hated that. The whole ballpark booed this guy who'd leaned over and snatched the ball. But you know, I've seen it happen dozens of times. It's remarkable how often the chance to grab his own major league ball can warp a man's sense of what's best for the home team. This guy who had reached over the box-seat railing had a Rush cap on; he was probably as staunch a Rushian as there was. But seeing that ball bouncing right to him had aroused an instinct more powerful than team loyalty.

I know he wished he hadn't done it. First off, he got his face slapped by the lady in the next seat to him. Nobody sympathized with him; he was a disgrace. And when Biela lined out to Grim to strand the runners, Rush-Cap became the focal point of an altercation down there in the left-field boxes. A fan behind him put a chokehold on him until the ushers came. They hauled Rush-Cap up the aisle so he wouldn't have to go on trying to explain himself. I noticed that they chose not to grab the guy who was applying the chokehold; it was clear who they thought the real troublemaker was.

But it could've happened to anybody; it's in the blood to catch the ball when you see it coming. There's only one exception to that rule and we got to witness it shortly.

Meanwhile, Jay's boys were out again. Everybody was kind of stunned. Nine hits in two innings, but no runs. The crowd was acting like they'd had their meat snatched away, and I thought to myself, well, this is curious.

During the top of the third, while Ron Amalfimatanio mowed us down again, Davy Tremayne stood at the home-plate end of our dugout, chewing sunflower seeds and gazing at Fabian Koonce from time to time. Fabian was sitting on our bench with a towel around his neck, taking deep gulps of air through his mouth and wiping his glasses off and kind of living alone. Nobody was sitting anywhere near him, but all the guys were peering at him now and then, just to see what a true oddity looked like. Then they'd focus on Davy and wonder when in the hell he was going to take him out. It wasn't as though Davy hadn't been warned by events that Fabian was ineffective. His Solidity Index must have been enormous.

Behind me on the Rush bench, Jay was bitter and disconsolate. "We had our chance," I heard him say to somebody at one point. "Now he'll bring in Seeburger, and Seeburger at least knows what he's doing. Timing is fuckin' all."

Earlier in the season when I was still with the Rush, Jay had illustrated his theory of timing for me. "Once when I was a teenager," he'd said, "I had a chance to catch the little Dallesandro brother out on the street and beat the shit out of him, but I had to hurry before the *big* Dallesandro brother showed up and beat the shit out of *me*. The old story. I couldn't catch the little one fast enough to stay out of the way of the big one. Timing is fuckin' all."

Jay was sure he'd missed his opportunity with Fabian Koonce, but he was wrong. Fabian was on the hill again in the bottom of the third. Davy sent him back to the mound, saying, "You're the worst, kid; get out there and pitch."

When Darrell Paris led off for the Rush in the third, he introduced the fans to an extra element in tonight's game: physical fear.

The matchup between Fabian Koonce and Darrell was unfair. Fabe was outclassed from here to there and back again. Paris just waited at the plate, swinging the bat easily through the strike zone, looking out at the mound with a gentle, open expression on his face, a little solemn, like a small boy watching his dad talk to a cop. He always looked like that, batting. His face was shy and his swing was brutal.

There was no suspense in anybody's mind about whether Paris could hit Koonce or not. He was obviously sure to mash anything Fabe threw up there. The only question was where it would go, and if Darrell could wait long enough on the ball to hit it fair.

He hit six or seven screaming buzzbombs foul before he finally singled to right, and by the time he'd hit the third one he had the undivided attention of every customer on the first-base side of the stadium. He raked the boxes on each swing, and the spectators who didn't look out were in considerable danger. At least one guy who'd been in the process of putting a hot dog in his mouth ate a baseball instead. The womenfolk screamed and the menfolk stepped aside when Darrell batted against Fabian Koonce.

Darrell was lefthanded and pulled everything Fabian served up, so the fans down the left-field line were pretty safe when he was hitting. But the target area changed when John Turk and Angelo Fanzone got up there, because they were righties and just as strong as Paris. It was the first game I can recall being at where I could see hundreds of onlookers physically flinch on every pitch.

This was the exception to that little rule about fans trying to catch any ball hit toward them. They will try to catch a ball, but not a bullet, and Jay's power hitters really strafed the seats in the bottom of the third. The hot dogs and beers were flying and the people were throwing their hands up and leaning over and shrieking while the foul shots ricocheted from customer to customer. Fabian's pitches were so fat and crippled that Paris, Turk and Fanzone were bashing them at almost right angles.

This endangered Sunset Boone, who, being seated just beyond the Rush dugout, had to dodge some of Turk's and Angelo's hardest shots. As a little boy I used to root for Sunset in his movies when he was hunkered down behind the rocks with the bad element blazing away at him. He used to get his Stetson shot right off his head. One of Fanzone's drives came whizzing at him just like that, but Sunset hadn't lost his Old Wrangler's reflexes; he got his head down just in time and the ball pulverized a little guy behind him who'd been trying to get back to his seat balancing four Cokes on a cardboard tray.

This was something a little different for everyone present. Box-seat fans have always known to keep an eye open for hard fouls, but in other games it's an infrequent occurrence. In *this* game, with Fabian Koonce in there, the fans were actually pinned down in their seats by their own hitters.

And it wasn't just the fans who were stuffing their heads down into their collarbones. When the Rush hitters got on base they had to do it too.

Paris got thrown out at third on Turk's single to center, but Turk got there safely when Fanzone finally hit one fair, doubling down the line in left. John took a walking lead off third with one out and Joe Surface almost decapitated him with a liner that hooked foul. Turk picked himself up, decided "Screw this," walked back to third and wouldn't lead off anymore no matter how much Jay yelled at him from the dugout.

John Turk was one of the most *basic* guys on the Rush; he'd told me once that he didn't "waste time analyzing things." I'm sure he'd never concerned himself much with subjects like physics, but he must have done some quick mass-times-velocity-plus-Koonce computations over on third, because he stayed right on the bag for the remainder of Surface's at-bat. With Fabian throwing Chuck-and-Duck, John wanted that whole ninety feet to react in.

While Jay hollered, *"Wait* on it!" at him over and over, Surface got a slow, loopy curve from Fabian, counted ten and took the hardest swing of his life, one of those that start back by the umpire's foot and continue until the batter screws himself into the ground. Naturally, he lifted his head halfway through. He was looking at the moon when he hit the ball, and that was about where it went—straight up the chute, past the ozone layer, out of my sight and into the night, a magnificent pop-up. Surface cursed a streak all the way down to first; we all had time to write home before it came down.

Nobody caught the ball; it landed on the mound. Fabian got out of the way, as he was supposed to do, but neglected to indicate for anyone in particular to take it. All our infielders stood in a circle and watched it thud onto the hill. Tremayne picked it up. With one out, the runners were standing on their bases. It looked like the game had stopped so we could all ponder this meteorite that had landed among us. The official scorer gave Surface a single.

The bases were loaded with Gonder up, and Tom drilled a few more fouls off the spectators before he lined one that Garry Perry dived for and speared backhanded. Then Garry rolled over, sat up and threw to second to double Fanzone off the bag, ending the inning.

As the Rush took the field for the fourth and our players came into the dugout, Perry looked up into the stands, where the box-seat fans were checking for broken bones and irregular heartbeats, and said to Slip Washington, "Maybe when Koonce is pitching we oughta use a Nerf."

20

"PEOPLE TALK ABOUT *ME* BEING CRAZY, BUT it's *Tremayne* who's the lunatic."

Jay was confiding in me at just under a scream from his dugout during the top of the fourth while his ace, Amalfimatanio, methodically retired our hitters. Ronnie hadn't given up a hit yet, and the score was still 0–0.

"He's managing worse than *you* would," said Jay, so exasperated he was willing to yell his troubles to me. "Has he *forgotten* who's pitching? I never left a guy in who gave up thirteen hits in three innings."

"He ain't losin'," I said to Jay over my shoulder after Garry Perry grounded weakly to third.

"So you think it's smart?" Jay asked, ignoring the game, up on the top step of the dugout. "You think it's good baseball? Explain it to me, mastermind. Did we come into the game with thirteen more good breaks than you had all year, is that it? Are the *breaks* evening up, Charlie? What's fuckin' next, a shit-rain on my head?"

"Want your jacket, Jay?" I heard Leo Keeler ask, while Davy Tremayne got our first hit, a single to the hole at short.

"*No,* I don't want my jacket!" said Jay. "I want a goddamn *run!* Remember those? Remember when we used to score *runs?* Remember yesterday, when we got ten fuckin' *runs?*"

Keeler said, "Jay, if it's all right with you I'm gonna wear a batting helmet out there next time Turk and Fanzone come up, just in case. I mean I'm pretty close to 'em and they just jump all over everything Koonce throws up there."

Jay said, "I don't care if you wear a slit skirt."

Casale hit into a double play and Fabian came out to pitch the bottom of the fourth.

As I watched the Rush lose one man on a pickoff by Hartman, another trying to stretch a hit, and then load the bases and strand all three on a warning-track drive to Washington, it occurred to me that maybe they and Jay were trying too hard. I've found in day-to-day situations around the house that certain things won't respond to the aggressive approach. I'm referring to stuck drawers and windows and doorlocks and such; I tend to lose patience with them when they don't give right away and then I pull and push and yank on them harder and harder until they break, or I'm tired, or until Pat comes up and gives them a little sideways jiggle and gets them to open or turn or whatever it is they're supposed to do. And it struck me that my problem of trying to force inanimate objects to work at home might be similar to Jay trying to force runs in a ballgame by pushing runners forward without realizing that a calmer, more conservative approach might work better.

I chose not to suggest this to Jay, though. You don't advise the enemy, and besides he probably would've taken it as another instance of someone telling him to take it easy.

Jay was in an extra hurry to make things happen because he still believed Koonce would be leaving the game any minute for somebody good. But after the fourth inning, Davy didn't even have anyone warming up in the pen.

It was now clear to me that Davy didn't think like other managers. He didn't even think like other *hunch* managers. A hunch manager would have removed Fabian by this time, on the hunch that he was horrible. But Fabian was Davy's special pick, and Davy didn't renege on those picks often. He'd spent his whole career thinking, "This will come out right because I'm Davy Tremayne." Or rather, not Davy Tremayne, but Rex the Flex Plexstra or Stwint Fwenton or whoever he was using to cheat the circumstances at that particular moment. Only now, instead of becoming an imaginary person to give himself real ability, he was using real people whose *ability* was imaginary.

And in an odd way, so far, Fabian Koonce was proving him right. He was certainly special. He wasn't worth spit but he wasn't losing, either, and with each inning that went by we were chipping away at Jay's temper like a jackhammer pounding pavement.

After four innings, the Rush had eighteen hits and no runs. It seemed to me there was no way they could go on getting four and five hits an inning without scoring. And I was right. The next time they batted they made history.

Fanzone led off with a leg double but overslid second headfirst and Davy tagged him out. Surface singled, took a big leadoff and Hartman picked him off. Gonder and Miranda singled and Amalfimatanio chopped one straight down in front of the plate and beat it out to load the bases.

So—two out, bases drunk again, no score, crowd screaming, J. W. Shain up, Koonce working on a twenty-three-hitter.

Here again, a good spot to remove the man who has proven to everyone's satisfaction that he hasn't got it. But Davy didn't. He didn't even come in from second to talk to Fabian. He was like those people who keep smoking cigarettes in the face of overwhelming medical evidence.

The fans were *begging* for a clutch hit by this time, and J.W., already three for three, ripped a couple fouls down the right-field line and worked the count full.

On three and two with two out, the runners are supposed to move with the pitch. Had *I* been the runner on third, I would've refused, as John Turk had earlier. Tom Gonder, though, was always willing to take a chance. It was he who had kissed the pavement when he slid off Surface's car in spring training. He was tough and brave and, I would say, reckless to the point of stupidity, and as Fabian delivered the three-and-two pitch to Shain he galloped several feet down the line from third.

J.W. had made up his mind to wait on the ball no matter how long it took to get there, and he waited until the pitch had almost floated past him. Then he took a vicious slap-swing at it and drilled it directly into Tom Gonder's groinal area.

Well, that cup the boys wear down there affords *some* protection, but it's not a fortress. You feel a shot like that at close range. Gonder kind of folded over himself and went down on his knees and pressed his forehead into the baseline while the crowd gave one of those collective, involuntary gasps: "OHHHH!" I'm sure every man in the stands clenched his lap. We all came out onto the field to look at Tom. Players are always eager to see how somebody is going to handle a catastrophe like temporarily acquiring a third ball.

Gonder was speechless. The two trainers decided to wait a couple minutes before they even moved him. Eventually they took him back to the Rush clubhouse, carrying him in the same curled-up position he went down in; he seemed to prefer to remain that way.

There was a delay while it was determined whether Gonder would be coming back, and guys from both teams sort of milled around near the mound for a couple minutes, talking over what had happened.

Shain's ball was an automatic hit, and Tom was an automatic out, so the Rush had managed to pile up six hits in the inning without pushing a runner over the plate. That feat made a big impression on the little cluster of people I found myself in, which included Jay, Darrell Paris and Ray Kazanski.

"That's a first, isn't it? Isn't that a first?" Kazanski asked me. "That's gotta be a first. Six hits and no runs in an inning."

"I didn't think it was possible," I admitted. "You know, if that happened every inning, Koonce could pitch a fifty-four-hit shutout."

"He's the guy to do it, right, skip?" said Paris. Jay was staring stonily at Tremayne, who was in another group of players, and didn't answer.

I was still turning it over in my mind. "You wouldn't

think a pitcher could throw a hit to every batter in an inning and not give up any runs," I said. "Ordinarily if you don't get anybody out it's an infinite number of hits and an infinite number of runs, right? Wouldn't it be?"

I looked at Jay, who looked back at me without moving, biting down on the insides of his cheeks. After a moment he said clearly, "I think it would be a whole lot better if you stopped talkin' like Professor Whizdick."

"Y'know what this is like?" said Paris. "Playing against Koonce is like the toughest lay in history. We're hard as logs but we just can't get *in*."

Tom Gonder finally returned to the game, exciting universal admiration. He seemed more subdued than usual. I went out to my coaching position for the top of the sixth, still thinking about the possibility of a fifty-four-hit shut-out. It couldn't happen tonight, of course, but until tonight it had never dawned on me that it could *ever* happen: a game in which the pitcher did absolutely everything wrong and still had it come out right. A basic counterdiction, Jay might say. It had taken Fabian Koonce to show us all that there was room in the rules for such a game. He was like a great inventor or pioneer, opening our eyes to whole new vistas of ineptitude, out there on his own in unmapped territory.

I noticed that the hard-core fans, the Rushians, were starting to have all kinds of difficulty accepting what was going on. Lungs was completely at sea. After the six-hit inning he just screamed out, "What the fuck *IS* this?" and didn't get any response from his neighbors.

*   *   *

By the time we got through the fifth our own players had partially dropped the idea that Davy was crazy to leave Koonce in there. They knew that however it turned out, they were in the middle of a game that had never come before. It was kind of moving to see the way they would look at Davy and Fabian in the dugout—awed, like they were a couple of magicians.

We did have one guy who was upset about the way things were going, though. Ted Grim, our third baseman, was a devout religious type, I'm not sure what denomination. He was interested in purity, I know that—purity of soul and body. Ted liked to get up before dawn and run fifteen miles and then drink some spring water. I've never seen anyone in better condition. He looked too perfect to be a baseball player; he looked like he should be reclining on one elbow touching fingers with God.

I think to Teddy the body was a temple and the earth was a temple too, and the mind was supposed to be a temple. He was admirable in every way as far as I was concerned, but I didn't hang around him much because he made me feel uncomfortable and not quite up to the mark. Maybe you know how it is. Some religious people will still sit around and joke with you, and some won't. Teddy Grim was aptly named.

Anyway, the game as it proceeded through the fifth got to disturbing Teddy on some level I don't quite understand. He came up to Davy Tremayne in our dugout before the sixth and said, "The pattern of this game is evil, skip."

Davy looked at him and then up at the stands, where some of the fans were howling over their team's inability to push one over, and said, "What's wrong with it?"

"I think maybe Koonce is under some kind of satanic influence," said Grim. "He's pitching almost the negative image of a perfect game. It's like the Anti-Game."

Davy didn't have a rejoinder for that one; he treated himself to a new handful of sunflower seeds and finally said, "Oh, yeah?"

"I don't feel right playing any longer in a game I think has a devilish quality to it," said Grim.

Davy gazed at him for a second and then gave me a look as if to say, "Find this one in the manager's manual." Then he called down the bench for Andy Macy, our best utility infielder.

When Macy came over, Davy said, "Andy, Ted here has to leave the game 'cause it's against his religion to play in a twenty-four-hit shutout. You loose?"

"Sure," said Macy, glancing at Grim, who stood there looking unshakable.

"You got any standards or beliefs that would keep you from playing third base?" Davy asked.

Macy obviously hadn't thought about it. "I guess not," he said dubiously.

"Good, you're in there. Teddy, I want you to know I respect your right to come up with these ideas. But I don't want you bothering Koonce, making the sign of the cross at him or anything, okay?"

Grim walked away, and Davy said to me, "If this game's doin' that to him, it's probably doin' it to some of them," and indicated the rest of the stadium.

*   *   *

The line score for the sixth, seventh and eighth innings might seem to indicate that Fabian Koonce settled down during that time, because the Rush only got two hits. But the truth was that they hit the ball just as hard as ever; nearly all their drives were either "at-'em" balls or caught by one of our fielders after a run and a dive. Three shots in a row were gloved in the sixth, and afterward Jay Bates moaned, "Oh, Christ, don't tell me he's getting the fuckin' *hang* of it."

The Rush hitters kept hammering the ball to no effect in the seventh and eighth, and the atmosphere in the ballpark began to get like it does in Missouri just before a tornado. I remember that when Jay took a bat to the Rush water cooler during the eighth and smashed at it until the bat broke—and then continued the process with another bat—nobody in the dugout, none of the umpires, nobody at all went over to ask him to stop. Everyone considered it suitable behavior. He was only doing to the cooler what a lot of fans wanted to do to him and us.

The Rushians had suffered enormously through the first eight, and they blamed three people—Fabian Koonce, Davy Tremayne and Jay, who'd been their hero when the game started. They were down on Jay for running his players into so many tags, and their attitude toward Fabian and Davy was somewhere on the far side of intense dislike. Looking at those fans, you could just about see the mercury rising up their necks and faces to the bills of their Rush caps.

And why not? Of the 38,000-plus in the stands, 38,000-plus were convinced that *they* could hit Fabian Koonce, and they couldn't get over the fact that Davy was leaving him in and getting away with it. In the late innings they wouldn't even cheer their players when they came up; they'd just sit there, waiting for something to go wrong. When it did, they'd all growl, like a giant bear getting poked with a stick. It made us uneasy on the field. There are better ways to spend an evening than whipping thousands of people up into a rage.

By the ninth, Sunset Boone and Jessup had decided they'd prefer to watch the finish from the glassed-in booth up near the press box. I think they felt too exposed to hard fouls and cranky neighbors down there where they'd been.

Looking back, I'd say that a plot or chart of the general state of mind of the crowd as the game progressed would go this way, gauging their feelings just after each inning:

> 1st—Disappointed
> 2nd—Sore at Rush-Cap for interfering with ball
> 3rd—Scared of fouls
> 4th—Frustrated
> 5th—Shocked (six-hit inning)
> 6th—Mad
> 7th—Madder
> 8th—Hold my coat

We went into the ninth still tied, 0–0. Fabian Koonce had a twenty-six-hitter.

As the ninth inning began, prominent among the people at the park who had lost their temper was Ronnie Amalfimatanio. He'd been in pitchers' duels before, but never like this.

Gee, he pitched a good game. He shut us down completely for eight innings. Minimal justice demanded that he be ahead of Koonce, but he wasn't, and Ron was mightily pissed off. He'd seen his teammates play pinball on the bases for most of the night and all he had to show for it was a two-hitter and a tie. Standing out there as the inning began, he looked like he knew he was ultimately going to get it in the rear.

Finally he started to give. We loaded the bases with one out, and with Davy up, Jay went out to the mound to talk to him. The crowd went into a medium fit. This was the first opportunity they'd had to see Jay out on the field where they could tell him what they thought of his early-inning tactics. So they all offered their opinion while he talked to Amalfimatanio and then walked back to the bench through a shower of debris from the stands.

After it got cleaned up, Davy stood in at the plate and Ronnie flipped him with a fastball. A risky thing to do with the bases loaded, but I guess Jay had him do it as a gesture of defiance or something. It was a good duster; Davy went down without his bat and his cap and the ball barely missed him. Gonder stabbed it and the crowd cheered on general principles.

But strategically it was unsound, because it cut into Ronnie's margin for error. Davy Tremayne was no longer a great hitter, but he was the right man for that spot. He fought off several of Amalfimatanio's best pitches, fouling them, and finally worked him for a walk. It forced in a run and we led, 1–0.

The Rushians didn't like it, and neither did Ron. He yanked his cap down so hard on his head that it must have impeded the circulation to his brain, because he threw a high slider to John Casale, who loves high sliders. When he laced it to left for a two-run single, it sent some of the fans around the bend. I saw one customer biting his own arm in the box seats over first, just chomping away; it was terrible.

Davy made it to third on the hit, called time and said to me, "When the inning's over, tell everybody—especially Koonce and the outfielders—if we get them out in the ninth we're sprinting for the runway."

This to me was the most sensible piece of strategy Davy had come up with all night. I'd never felt anywhere near as unpopular as I did right then, with my St. Louis uniform on.

Kazanski hit into a double play and we took a three-run lead into the bottom of the ninth.

21

DON'T COME AROUND ME WITH THAT STUFF
about how California fans leave the game early. None
of *these* fans did. They were militant. They wanted something done.

The Santa Rita cops had expected a big night at the
ballyard and there were quite a few of them standing
before the foul lines when the inning started in case some
of the spectators wanted to hop onto the field after the
game. But they *hadn't* expected to see so many people
moving down toward the front of the boxes; a whole pile
of fans came down the aisles and over the seats toward
the diamond to get a closer look, and the ushers didn't
seem to care to try to stop them. The Rushians were all
crammed down there in the front as the bottom of the
ninth began, with the cops near the lines. And there was
a lot of screaming, of course. They had progressed beyond
growling.

I'd like to say a few quick words here about Fabian
Koonce. He'd been going through quite an experience.
He really was trying his best. As the game had gone on
his face had gotten redder and redder, I think from

embarrassment. If he could've struck just one guy out it would have done wonders for his self-esteem, and the crowd might've found things easier to accept. But I don't think I'd even seen a Rush hitter swing at a single pitch and miss it all night.

I'll say one thing for him—his control was good. I was happy to have been right about that. He didn't walk anybody.

Well, when you've already given up twenty-six hits you don't worry too much about working the corners anymore. You just serve it up there. So Turk sent a rope right back up the middle and the Rush had their leadoff man on first.

Here Jay demonstrated that he was still yanking on the doorknob by calling for the hit-and-run. Now that's generally considered to be rockhead baseball, down three runs, but Jay had been pulling similar plays all season. Turk took off and had the base stolen, but Fanzone belted another liner up the middle and hit him with it as he slid into second. One out, another hit, Fanzone on first. At which point Davy had our first baseman do the hidden-ball trick.

It was real easy. Jay's own players were so busy booing him that they weren't paying attention. Davy called a conference at the mound and handed the ball to Kazanski, and when the meeting broke up and Fanzone led off first, Ray tagged him out.

Oh, Jesus, then the fans yelled; they lost it. They started throwing belts and pants and shoes and everything onto the field. One guy threw another guy. We were sufficiently terrified that Davy tried talking to the umps. He wanted a forfeit because of the crowd but he didn't get it.

I saw Koonce turn around on the mound and look out toward center during the long time-out the umps took to clear people's clothing off the field, so I went out to talk to him. When I got there he was looking up at the little scoreboard in center, up where it had the Rush totals: Runs, 0, Hits, 28."

"Fabian," I asked him, "is there anything you haven't tried?"

He didn't reply, evidently lost in thought, and out of the corner of my eye I saw Jay Bates walking slowly past me. He was approaching Davy Tremayne, who was talking to an ump out behind second. I decided to catch up with Jay.

He knew it was me when I got up to him, although he didn't look at me. He just kept walking toward Tremayne, saying, "I'm not gonna do anything." When he got to Davy he stopped, and Davy nodded at him.

Jay wasn't wild or raving or anything like that. He looked uncertain, like he needed a big favor and didn't know if it was right to ask.

He said quietly, "When the game's over, you'll give me a chance to get at you, won't ya? I just want to . . . *see* you after the game."

Davy didn't look too happy about it, but it seemed only fair. He chewed his sunflower seeds and finally said, "Sure, Jay."

Jay nodded, relieved, and turned around and walked back through the noise from the crowd.

Sunset Boone's voice came over the PA and asked the

fans to remember the game wasn't over and anybody who came out onto the field would be making an unlawful assemblage of himself. Things finally settled down enough so Fabian could pitch to Joe Surface with two out and nobody on.

Fabian was composed. He threw his first pitch directly over the plate, as so many others had been, and Surface lined it to right for a base hit. Then Gonder smashed one through the hole at short and Marty Miranda followed with a single to left to load the bases again. While all this happened the fans never made a sound. In our dugout, I wondered whether the cops had tear-gas canisters or stun guns or what. I didn't think it would matter much what they had if the next hitter caromed one off another runner.

Well, the due batter was Amalfimatanio, and he looked back at Jay from the on-deck circle, expecting to get pulled for a pinch-hitter, but Jay wasn't really in the game at that moment. He was sitting, staring out at Davy Tremayne, and taking a deep, shuddering sigh. So Amalfimatanio shrugged and walked up to the plate.

But a few seconds before Fabian pitched to Ron, Darrell Paris finally got Jay's attention on the bench by slapping him a few times. Jay woke up, looked at the mound and home plate and realized his pitcher was batting with the bases loaded and two out, down three runs in the bottom of the ninth.

Now like most pitchers, Ronnie wasn't a very good hitter, but then with Koonce pitching he didn't have to be. He was big and strong and extremely mad, and on

Fabian's first pitch, he hit one out of the park to left. Oh, he juiced it.

The thing was, I'd seen Jay wave at the home-plate umpire just before the pitch was thrown, and Jay had called time. He'd decided at the last moment that he wanted a pinch-hitter. The ump had seen Jay's gesture and raised his arms, stepping away from the plate as the pitch came in, so the grand-slam homer that won the game and the division for the Rush, 4–3, didn't count.

The crowd didn't realize it right away. They were cheering and screaming for the homer while Davy frantically waved our outfielders in. I ran out there, straight to the mound, and grabbed Koonce by the arm. I didn't have to be John McGraw to sense what was going to happen when the fans found out Jay had invalidated their pennant.

"It didn't *count!*" Fabian said as I pulled at his arm.

"It doesn't *matter!*" I yelled at him. "Come *on,* we gotta *go!*"

The crowd was gradually realizing from the way the umps were acting that something had gone wrong again. The umps were signaling for the Rush runners to go back to their bases. Not that they did—the runners knew, like we did, that the call wasn't going to go over.

A voice came over the PA and announced, "The umpires have ruled that since the Rush manager called time prior to the last pitch, the home run is nullified."

As last straws go, it was pretty heavy. There was a kind of rising roar from the Rushians and—I'm sure you've seen crowds do what they call "the wave" in the stands. This crowd *became* a wave. They went over the top.

Not everybody jumped out onto the field at first, but a goodly number surged over the railings all around us. If I had to speculate on who in particular they were mad at, breaking it down like one of those Gallup Polls, I'd say that in a random sample of 100 fans on the field, 15 were after the home-plate ump, 25 resented Fabian Koonce, 50 held either Davy Tremayne or Jay Bates or both responsible, and 10 were just out there looking for adventure. There were some Undecideds still up in the stands and they were throwing things. The game wasn't officially over, but we could tell it was over for a *while,* at least. It had definitely peaked.

Jay was a man with a mission, too; he broke out of the Rush dugout in front of the fans and headed directly for Tremayne, who was between first and second waving his players toward our runway. Jay had a bat in his hand, so even the fans most critical of his managing weren't coming right up to him to tap him on the shoulder. The ones who were able to get past the cops kind of followed him, fanned out behind.

When people are running around in an anarchic way and screaming and yelling and tackling each other with even less organization than you see on a junior-high-school kickoff return, things happen much faster than you can really take in. I remember my son Jamie took his first ride on a motorcycle when he was six, sitting in front of my next-door neighbor while he took a trip around the block at about twenty miles per hour. When Jamie got back to me, he took off his bicycle helmet and panted a little and said, "I thought I was going at the speed of life." These folks on the field were moving at the "speed of life," and it was scary. A real mob moves much more quickly than, say, a mob of extras in a movie, and they go in all directions at once. I can only recall flashes of what I saw.

I know I had pulled Fabian pretty close to our dugout when I first noticed Jay approaching Davy, and I must have stopped and stood still for a few seconds because I have the same vantage point in my memory for the next series of images:

I saw Davy become aware of Jay when they were about thirty feet apart. Upon seeing the bat in Jay's hand, Davy got a look on his face corresponding to saying, "Uh-oh."

I saw Davy start toward the dugout.

I saw Jay veer to cut him off.

I seem to remember moving toward them, thinking that out of duty to the game I should try to keep one manager from bludgeoning the other.

I saw Davy go down on his knees suddenly.

It happened so fast that I thought maybe he'd been shot. One second he was up and the next he was kneeling, sitting on his heels near first base, looking confused.

I looked at Jay, thinking somehow *he'd* done it. But Jay had stopped cold. He was stupefied. Neither of us had ever seen anything go awry with Tremayne, and when Davy teetered on his knees and then went over sideways, we couldn't believe it. It was unnatural.

So Jay froze for a second, and then he, Fabian and I ran and got to Davy together, ahead of the fans, who were all over the place tussling with cops and park security. By this time I was *sure* he'd been shot, but I was wrong. As we stood over him, Jay bent down and picked up something off the ground next to him. It was a size D battery, like from a flashlight—an Energizer, I believe.

Somebody had thrown it, probably from the stands, and it had caught Davy on the side of the head when he wasn't looking, which was the only way you *could* catch Davy. Who would do such a thing? Well, lots of people would. I've noticed before that when fans throw things at the ballpark, batteries are often included.

Fabian Koonce and I each took an arm and began dragging Davy toward our dugout. Some gigantic fan came barreling at us from the side and was about to run over all three of us when Jay swung his bat lefthanded— rather smoothly; he didn't overstride—and got the guy on the hip. The fan spun around and hobbled out of our lives. I didn't feel sorry for him. These customers can say what they want from their seats, but they lose my sympathy when they rush the stage.

I was glad Jay had chosen to ride shotgun for us while we pulled Davy off the field, but it wasn't as surprising as you might think. In this kind of crisis, men from both teams instinctively band together, back to back, in the tradition of entertainers all down through time who've had to defend themselves after putting on a really bad show.

Fabian and I pulled Davy along while his feet moved kind of aimlessly; his eyes were open but not alert. By the time we got to our dugout the other players had made it to shelter on one side of the field or the other, bowling over fans where they had to. People were still running over the diamond but they weren't organized;

there were a couple of pileups near home plate and the pitcher's mound. Hurricane Hartman was standing guard at the entrance to our runway with a bat in his hands. Fabian and I hauled Davy past him, Jay following.

When we got a few steps into the runway, we propped Davy up against the concrete wall and took a breather. Behind us, beyond Hurricane and the dugout steps, it was noisy. At the other end of the runway was the entrance to our locker room, which was closed. For the moment the four of us were alone.

Jay was exhilarated. "Did you see the way I hit that moke?" he said, replaying his swing against the opposite wall of the runway. "Full extension. Right on the bone. Liner up the alley." He dropped the bat and focused on Davy, and so did I.

Davy didn't focus back too well. His eyes weren't right; they were placid and kind of dreamy. He had a tendency to try to sit down but I didn't want him to. He looked past me with a "Bless-you-my-son" expression at Jay, who was now taking the battery out of his hip pocket and staring at it.

"How about that?" Jay said, palming the battery and making a fist around it. "First time I ever saw *anything* happen to you, Tremayne. I think you finally squeezed all your luck outta the tube." Jay came closer to Davy, right up behind me, and put his left hand on Koonce's shoulder, saying, "You choked up tonight, keepin' this popover in the game, didn't ya? And I beat ya, too. I don't care what the umps say." Satisfied with his grip on the battery, he grinned at Davy and added, "Now I'm gonna do it again."

I stood taller in front of Jay, thinking, "This is absolutely the last time I'm going to do this." Koonce joined me.

I said, "Jay, the guy's hurt. He's not right. You can't slug a guy with a concussion."

"I'll be *happy* to," said Jay.

"He doesn't even know what's goin' *on*," I said. "*Look* at him."

Jay did, suspiciously. Davy smiled and sighed happily. Jay kept peering at him over my shoulder.

"Who are you?" Jay asked finally.

"Shoot, *you* know who he is," said Fabian.

"Shut up, Koonce," said Jay. "And don't coach him." Jay reached over my shoulder and poked Davy in the collarbone with his extended fingers. "Hey. Who are you?"

Davy blinked, made an effort to stand up straighter and said with dignity, "David Tremayne . . . author and statesman." I thought, what a horrible time to give his right name for a change. He was like a shell of his former selves.

Jay had started his right arm back on "David Tremayne," and both Fabian and I had gotten ready to try and block him off, but on "author and statesman" Jay stopped and looked at Davy again, started the arm back and stopped it again, and lowered it. Squinting into Davy's eyes, he asked, "Who am *I?*"

Davy looked embarrassed, like he hadn't done his homework. He concentrated, searching Jay's face and uniform, and finally said, with some relief, "Well, you're an American, I can see that."

Jay exploded. "I'm Jay *Bates,* you dizzy prick! You

been chewin' on my liver for twenty years! You don't *know* me?" He looked at me and then back at Davy. "Is he faking? Is this some of his man-of-a-thousand-faces bullshit?"

I didn't think so. I couldn't be sure, because we were dealing with a man who'd always been versatile, but I could see on Davy's temple where the battery had hit him and it had made an indentation, and there was swelling and discoloration around it already. He was genuinely woozy. He now looked surprised and said, "I'm'na throw up."

All the blood went out of his face and he sank into a sitting position on the runway floor, leaning up against the wall, while Jay stared at him, flabbergasted.

"Sonofabitch, he doesn't know me," he said tonelessly. "What the fuck is the point of caving his teeth in if he doesn't even know who's doing it?"

Fabian Koonce said solemnly, "Jay, if you're feelin' like you have to hit somebody, you can try me."

Jay raised his eyes to Fabian's face and surveyed him wearily. "Koonce," he said, "*any*body can hit *you.*"

He looked out toward the field, past Hurricane Hartman's back, where the noise was still considerable.

"I'm gonna go find an ump and see if it's a forfeit," he said.

"I'd go by way of our clubhouse if I were you," I said. "Those fans don't think you're a genius tonight."

Jay dismissed the warning. "Screw 'em," he said, flipping the battery and palming it again. "Those bastards can't intimidate *me.*" He started toward the field, then stopped, turned around and looked at Davy again, undecided.

"Maybe I oughta give him one little shot anyway, whaddya think?" he asked me.

"You oughta hope he recovers," I told him. "He's the secret of your success."

Jay looked at me, snorted once and left the field.

22

THERE'S THIS OLD SONG I HEARD A WOMAN SING in a blues club in Chicago years ago—the lyric is addressed to some guy who fouled up, and I don't recall much of it, but I've always remembered the last line of the verse, which is, "Honey, I think you made your move too soon."

It could be that when the Rushians stormed the ballfield on the night of the Last Game, they made *their* move too soon. At the time, of course, they felt provoked beyond endurance. Losing that game-winning homer was too much weight for them to carry; they couldn't stand it. But had they been able to stop and reflect, it might've dawned on them that Ron Amalfimatanio was still up, after all, and perfectly capable of launching another one out of the park. As it was, though, their misbehavior was too showy for the umpires to ignore, and Ronnie never got another swing that night.

We watched the rest of the riot on TV in our clubhouse while the trainer examined Davy, and it was unnerving to see what all was going on right outside our door. Fabian sat next to me with a dazed look on his face. I wondered if that Helen of Troy woman had had similar feelings, seeing whole armies of men hacking and hewing at each other: "All this over *me?*"

I was again struck by the difficulty of the job the media had to do—particularly, in this case, the video cameramen, who seem to take it as a point of honor to stay in the middle of things and get some good footage when anyone else would fall back and shoot the proceedings from the press box or a blimp where it was safe. A better man than I am was actually out there with a minicam right in the thick of things near the pitcher's mound, and he got some exciting stuff of people grunting and straining and hollering and swinging before his angle suddenly changed and he provided us with a view of the night sky above while a couple pairs of feet jumped over him at the speed of life.

Then we got the overall scene from the press box, looking down on the diamond, and I thought I saw Jay at one point in the lower righthand corner of the screen, wrestling a fan and asking a cop for directions.

Our trainer said Davy was concussed and took him back to the office. The rest of the players were rattled but unhurt.

"Is the game over, Charlie?" Fabian Koonce asked me.

The TV showed the beginnings of a fire out by the left-field wall.

"I imagine," I said.

"Did we win?"

"Well . . . yeah, unless they rule it a justifiable riot."

About an hour later when things got more under control, the local news people interviewed Sunset Boone and

Ralph Jessup in the owner's private box overlooking the field. That was when we heard the umps had declared the game a forfeit and awarded the victory to St. Louis. The reporters wanted to know what Sunset and Jessup thought of it all. Jessup looked a little gray on-camera, but Sunset was unruffled.

"Nahh, I'm not gonna contest it," Sunset said. "Our folks ran too wild out there, no question. And I don't condone that kind of behavior. Tell ya, though—had I been a younger man and not owned the ballpark I mighta joined 'em."

One of the newsmen said witnesses claimed Jay Bates had hit at least one fan with a bat on the field, and now nobody could find Jay at all. There was speculation that one of the fans might have taken him home for a souvenir, or maybe several fans took parts of him. The reporter asked Jessup for his reaction to that.

Old Ralph was a little quick to wash his hands of Jay, I thought. "Bates was told repeatedly that violent incidents would not be tolerated," he said. "If it's true he was using a bat out there, and if he's still alive, he's fired."

"Oh, back up a step, Ralph," said Sunset. "The boy was out there defending himself. Lemme tell you fellas somethin' about Jay Bates. History may not give him credit for a sunny disposition but he put this town on the map." He looked down at the field and added, "Hope it's still on the map tomorrow."

Somebody asked Sunset about the fans who had tried to burn down the left-field wall, and he said he'd been planning on knocking the wall down over the winter anyway. I don't think I've ever seen an owner less inclined to fly off the handle than Sunset Boone.

It was late that night before we got the okay to up-periscope and surface. And in the ensuing days I found out how wrong I'd been when I told Pat you always get a definite outcome in baseball. They've been sorting that Last Game out ever since.

You probably didn't notice, but we lost our pennant play-off with Pittsburgh. We played it in an interest vacuum. All anybody wanted to talk about was the Rush game. Maybe it was asking too much of an ordinary playoff confrontation to take the spotlight from one that had featured a riot and a fire and fifty injuries. Even in Pittsburgh it seemed like nobody cared; or maybe it was just us.

Davy Tremayne suffered from even more identity confusion than usual for a few days after the battery hit him, and was unable to manage us in the postseason—which was the way I think our front office wanted it, anyway. Ruling in his place were Taylor Cheney, the pitching coach, by virtue of his knowledge of our staff, and me, by virtue of my courage and heart. Davy was allowed to sit on the bench during the games; his doctors didn't see anything wrong with it. Nobody paid much attention to his strategic thinking, though; he'd kind of lost credibility during the Santa Rita game. I think the players half-expected him to stick a sail on our home dugout and try to pilot us down the left-field line and on out to the Mississippi.

All during the playoffs the experts were crawling all over the front pages of the sports section arguing about what the hell had happened in the Last Game and whose fault it was. First they wrote editorials on how the American sports fan was no more than a heathen. Then they talked about how Jay Bates was to blame for inciting the crowd with his kamikaze style. Finally, somebody came out with the theory that the reason for the riot was the crowd couldn't handle something as unfair as a thirty-one-hit shutout and the only way to prevent a possible recurrence was to change the rules of the game.

This individual went so far as to say the rules should be altered so that the team with most *hits* wins—and when his proposal actually received some consideration in the papers, I decided to take pen in hand. Talk about changing the rules just fries my butt. I honestly think I'd go to war over it.

There's nothing *wrong* with the rules, except of course for the DH; it just shows you how marvelously balanced they are, that there's room in them for a thirty-one-hit shutout, or even a *fifty-four*-hit shutout. The baseball rules are like a perfect circle with everything good and bad in it.

Of course, if a game like that makes people crazy it's not the kind of thing you want to *see,* but it's like I told Pat when I finally made it home—in a way that game had *value:* It showed where a crowd's absolute breaking point is. You know, they really were mighty patient. They didn't snap when their team had twenty-six hits and no runs, or twenty-eight, or thirty. They didn't truly lose their minds until they found out their game-winning grand-slam homer didn't count. It's testimony to the basic sporting nature of the people that they didn't try to demolish the place before they did.

And expecting that game to happen again is like thinking the next world war will be the same as the last one. You can't have that game without three individuals: Fabian Koonce, Jay Bates, and especially Davy Tremayne.

There's never really been any doubt in the minds of the baseball people as to who was responsible for that game being so screwy. It was Davy Tremayne and his magical mystical outlook. After the season was over Davy got called in for a meeting with the St. Louis higher-ups and they asked him gently why he pitched Koonce in the Last Game and why he stayed with him. I think Davy's reasoning struck them as chipped and peely because they've been in no hurry to announce his return as manager next year, suggesting instead that playing *and* managing might be too much of a strain on him.

Nobody who was looking for him saw Jay Bates until a week after the Last Game. He managed somehow to get out of the park alive that night without knocking anybody's block off and motored down to Tijuana, where he hung out with the railbirds at Agua Caliente for a few days, calling himself Jay-sus. He hadn't felt like listening to Jessup yell at him. When he came out of hiding, he found out he'd become a media giant. A videotape showed that the fan he'd hit with his bat had been about to run roughshod over Davy Tremayne, so that Jay had actually come to the rescue of his worst enemy—an act one writer compared to what the hero did in *A Tale of Two Cities*. The other fans in Santa Rita had forgiven him for calling time out before Amalfimatanio's home run, figuring, I guess, that they might have done the same.

There were *some* Rush fans who hadn't lost their bloodlust, but it was directed at Davy and Fabian Koonce, not Jay. I heard about some people in Santa Rita who were supposedly offering to track Davy and Fabian down and do away with them for a modest sum. That's just viciousness, you know; there's no place in baseball for the hunting down and extermination of your opponent. I used to tell Jay that.

But Jay himself is on velvet for the time being; he's the hottest thing since those little sticky pieces of paper that you can put on and take off of other pieces of paper. My grandmother Myrabelle Charles used to tell me the one sure way to be popular was to learn to play a musical instrument, but another sure way is to bring an expansion team to within a game of the playoffs in your first year. I got a call from Jay not too long ago and he told me Sunset had handed him a two-year contract with a raise and the light beer people were sending him flowers and candy. The Rush are the early-line favorites for next season. He called me up to thank me.

"Y'know, if I'da hammered Tremayne when I wanted to I coulda got in some runny shit," he said. "Now I'm the fair-haired boy. Jessup looks like a jerk for not backin' me up after the game. In two years *I'll* be GM; Boone loves my ass. And they're all sayin' Tremayne managed like a zombie—he'll be lucky to get renewed. Everybody hates *you* guys. It's like a fuckin' fairy tale."

There's no question Jay turned the corner career-wise
when he chose not to kill Davy. Some people even say
he's mellowed, but I was in the runway with him that
night and I'm not sure "mellowed" is the word. I'd still
rather read about him in the paper than work for him. But
Jay is like those dictators who get the trains running on
time—he'll always have a job as long as he doesn't break
international law.

I haven't heard from Davy except for a postcard from
some resort in the Caribbean; I guess those threats from
the Rush fans have kept him moving. In it he said he still
doesn't remember the aftermath of the game and that the
only chance for world peace is for all nations to be
abolished so that people can live under one flag. He drew
the flag on the postcard. He still seems a little disoriented
to me, but of course it's a lovely idea.

When a baseball season ends, the people on any given
team tend to separate fast, like billiard balls on the break.
I've only seen one St. Louis player since the finish of the
postseason, and that was Fabian Koonce.

Over the long Thanksgiving weekend Pat and Jamie
and I went down to LaPorte to visit my folks, and while
we were there I ran into Fabian in a hardware store in
West Quincy. He's got a little facial twitch now, comes
and goes about every thirty seconds or so. The rest of
him appears to be okay.

He said he'd gotten an offer from one of those Wild,
Wacky World of Sports TV shows to go back to Santa
Rita in February and restage Ron Amalfimatanio's final

at-bat to see what might have been. He didn't seem eager to return to the scene.

Fabian received his unconditional release from St. Louis as soon as he got home, which struck me as ungrateful of management but understandable. Giving up thirty-two hits in eight-and-two-thirds is evidence of unsuitability for your work even if the thirty-second doesn't count.

I asked him if he was thinking of trying to hook on with some other club and he said, "I don't believe I will. I think I've had sufficient."

He might be able to get a job as a batting-practice pitcher, though. Fact is, he could be the greatest batting-practice pitcher who ever lived.

He was kind of unhappy about having set such an odd record pitching in the Last Game, and asked me if I thought that someday, somebody might pitch a complete thirty-two-hit shutout and take the record away from him, get him off the hook. I told him anything was possible, but honestly, it looks to me like he might have one of those unbreakables.

As for me, I don't know yet exactly what I'm going to do. Pat thinks I should consider a future outside the game, because I've had a couple nightmares since returning home in which the Santa Rita crowd succeeds in getting into our locker room. But I don't want to leave baseball; I still love it. Bates-ball and Tremayne-ball have their flaws, but baseball remains perfect to me. And I think it needs me, or people like me who understand it and are willing to stand up for it the way it's constructed.

So when all this blows over, as I hope it will, and the game starts up again without those gimpy rules changes they've been hatching, I'll be making the rounds as a coach—to St. Louis first, if they'll have me. I know I can do something for some club, even if it's only hitting grounders for a kid shortstop until I've used up all my days and hours and minutes.

And even if I can't stay in organized ball I can always go out into the backyard and play catch with Jamie. He likes it and we get a little rhythm going, throwing it back and forth. It's healthy, I believe. You know, years ago my first manager, Fred Brice, was wrong when he told me what baseball would do to me. The game has always been *good* for my heart.

ABOUT THE AUTHOR

Sherwood Kiraly was born in 1949 and grew up in Illinois and Missouri. He worked for sixteen years at the national newspaper syndicate variously named Publishers-Hall, Field, News America and North America Syndicate, in Chicago and later in Irvine, California. His positions included Comics Editor and Managing Editor. He has written comedy for network television and occasional humor pieces for newspapers, and now lives in Laguna Beach, California, with his wife and two children. *California Rush* is his first novel.